SUFFERING
HUMAN AND DIVINE

GREAT ISSUES OF LIFE SERIES

THE ETERNAL GOSPEL
By Rufus M. Jones

CHRISTIANITY AND ECONOMICS
By Sir Josiah Stamp

THE CONTEMPORARY CHRIST
By The Very Rev. Richard Roberts

A TESTAMENT OF FAITH
By Dr. P. G. S. Hopwood

SUFFERING, HUMAN AND DIVINE
By Principal H. Wheeler Robinson

Forthcoming Volumes

IMMORTALITY
By Professor Eugene Lyman

THE BIBLE
By Professor James Moffatt

GOD
By Robert Calhoun

JESUS CHRIST
By Dr. C. H. Dodd

*Other Volumes in the Series Will
Be Announced Later*

SUFFERING
HUMAN AND DIVINE

BY

H. Wheeler Robinson, M.A., D.D.,

Principal of Regent's Park College, Oxford

Introduction by Rufus M. Jones

Editor of the Great Issues of Life Series

New York · 1 9 3 9

THE MACMILLAN COMPANY

PRINTED IN THE UNITED STATES OF AMERICA
AMERICAN BOOK—STRATFORD PRESS, INC., NEW YORK

INTRODUCTION

I KNEW when I asked Dr. H. Wheeler Robinson to write this volume on *Suffering* that I was giving him the most difficult task which this Series on Great Issues of Life would impose on any writer in the list. The problem of suffering was difficult enough in the days when the Book of Job was written, when the Psalmists faced the hard issues of life, when Milton tried to "justify the ways of God," when Leibnitz sounded the deeps and shallows of his philosophy. But we in these later times have opened many new doors in the vast house of the universe; we have peered into hidden closets; we have enlarged the area of knowledge, but at the same time we have widened the circumference of mystery.

The majestic order, the mathematical regularity, the unvarying precision, the immensity of the spaces and the time-spans convince our minds that this cannot be a realm of chaos or accident, but we are more than ever puzzled and brought to suspense by the terrible list of pains and perils which beset what we are prone to believe is the crowning work of creation, the topmost being that has yet appeared. He is so well constructed, so nobly provided for, so highly endowed, so full of longings and aspirations, so fitted for a world of a higher order than the physical and biological sphere, why is he not given greater security in his domain, why is he so beset with assaults and threats, with agonies and suffering, why are there these swarms of privileged microscopic enemies, why are there these hereditary traits which menace him, why is there the long historical trail of hindrances and frustration?

Professor W. Macneile Wilson, in his Gifford Lectures (1935-7), *The Human Situation*, has marshalled the facts of our human troubles and besetments so impressively and, I may say, so appallingly that no reader of his book can doubt that it is no easy undertaking to "heal the hurt" of the human race, or to justify man's trail of suffering, either from Nature or from History. One item from Professor Wilson's book suggests trouble enough to disturb our imagination and to give pause to our optimism. There are, he says, seven hundred million sufferers from malaria in the world, and that is only one of the woes that assaults the human family.

The author of this present book knows all about this side of the story, and more too. He has written with his eyes open on the whole picture. Sin is a darker mystery than malaria and he must deal with that. He undertook his task not lightly in ignorance, but seriously and bravely, knowing the depth and difficulty of it. He saw clearly from the first that there is no answer without coming to grips with the problem of a time-order, and without facing the still deeper questions of the nature of God and the mysterious fact of His suffering. The answer is not from the outside, from Nature inward, but rather from the inward discovery of Grace operating within us and beyond us, from the reality of resources actually at hand that enable a person to absorb pain and suffering without spoiling one's joy. "The peace we are seeking," this author tells us near the end of his book, "is not the peace of escape from the sufferings of life, but the peace of victory won in their very midst and through their endurance." He finds an allegory in the ritual of the Temple in Jerusalem: "It was the duty of a solitary priest to go in the darkness into the inner enclosure of the altar to clear away the ashes of the fire which was kept continually burning. It was the rule that 'none went with him and he carried no lamp, but he walked in the light of the altar fire.' My thought is that every man who goes on doing his duty in the darkness of suffering will be walking by the light of *some* altar fire, though none but himself may know of it, and perhaps not he himself."

INTRODUCTION

George Fox, at the opening of his career as the spiritual prophet of his period, had two experiences which steadied his faith and gave him unique marching power. "I saw," he said, "that there is an ocean of darkness and death, but I saw that there is an infinite Ocean of Light and Life and Love which flows over the ocean of darkness. In that I saw the infinite Love of God." In the other experience he saw the evils and frustrations of the world, what was out of tune and balance in the order of things, but he saw the "Light of Christ shine through all."

There is much of this same triumphant note in this book and though the persistent problem is not brought to a final solution and cannot be at this stage, this same Light from above "shines through all" and is the answer for those who can see it. The book is a fine blending of deep evangelical insight and clear understanding of modern scientific realism.

RUFUS M. JONES

PREFACE

A SMALL book on so great and familiar a subject labours under a serious disadvantage. So many such books have been written about suffering that anyone who refused to read another might well be excused. After all, what can be said that is new? what, indeed, can be said that is worth saying? Why not frankly admit that the perennial problem of suffering is insoluble?

Something of this was in my mind when the Editor of this series asked me to write on "The Problem of Suffering". I was reluctant to undertake the task, because aware that mere argument on such a theme cannot take us far. Yet, it can do something. Intellectual criticisms of divine providence must be countered on their own ground, in Bishop Berkeley's confidence that "The same Principles which, at first view, lead to Scepticism, pursued to a certain point, bring men back to Common Sense". So, only, the way is cleared for that more vital and personal reaction to life which we call "faith". We can bring God in, not as the premise of an argument, but as the rock on which we build. There is no intellectual solution of the prob-

lem of suffering which can give the comfort and
strength which the individual sufferer needs. But just
there, where the need is sorest, and through the very
need itself, the discovery can be made that God suffers in us, with us, for us. That is the only adequate
solution of the problem known to me.

This is why I promised to write a book, not on "The
Problem of Suffering", but on "Suffering, Human and
Divine". I shall try to give the familiar arguments for
what they are worth. But I am more concerned to
help the sufferer, if I may, to face suffering in his own
life or in the lives of others, in the spirit of a genuine
Christian faith, for which the ultimate principle is
Solvitur Patiendo—"live it through".

If, then, anyone who does read this book finds the
earlier chapters inadequate, as affording too partial
and too abstract a discussion of a subject that is ultimately a personal one, let him remember that they are
but stages in a continuous argument which is meant
to open out into the personal attitude indicated in the
closing chapter.

I have to thank my colleague, the Rev. A. J. D.
Farrer, for reading the typescript, and making useful
criticisms, and another colleague, the Rev. L. H.
Brockington, for reading the proof and making the
index. I am grateful to Mrs. Phyllis Taunton Wood
for some thoughtful suggestions, as well as to other

PREFACE

friends too numerous to mention by name. I am
also grateful to the following for permission to use
copyright material:—Messrs. Cassell & Co., Messrs.
Doubleday Doran, and Mr. Robert Hichens for the
quotations from his novel, "Mrs. Marden"; Messrs.
Heinemann, Messrs. Alfred Knopf, and Mrs. Flecker,
for the lines quoted from J. E. Flecker's "Hassan";
Messrs. Macmillan & Co, London, for the quotation
from A. C. Bradley's "Shakespearean Tragedy";
Messrs. T. & T. Clark for the quotation from H. R.
Mackintosh's "Sermons". If there is any other instance of quotation for which I should have sought
permission, I apologize for the oversight in advance.

H. WHEELER ROBINSON

Oxford
Easter, 1939.

CONTENTS

THE ARGUMENT OF THE BOOK

I. Shakespeare's "King Lear" suggests that spiritual is
more intense than physical suffering, that suffering
may be a consequence of moral evil, and that suffering can be transformed from an evil to a good. It is
impossible to review the whole range and variety of
human suffering, but we must face the facts honestly, without accepting a dualism of Nature and
God. Our individual reaction to the fact is of the
first importance, and pain may be our path to the
first real discovery of God.

II. The explanations of suffering which we habitually
hold will affect our personal reaction to the actual
experience of it. These explanations are found at different levels, which it is important to distinguish.
Thus, at the biological level, we find that pain can
be a danger-signal and a stimulus to "progress"; at
the moral level, character can be developed by it; at
the religious level we find both the greatest difficulties in forming a theory, and the greatest resources
for the actual endurance of suffering. As varieties of
extra-Biblical explanation, we may take Buddhism,
Stoicism and Christian Science (with which we may
contrast Psycho-therapy).

III. The explanations of suffering in the Old Testament
deserve special notice, because the problem was cen-

tral for the religion of Israel. Suffering is there explained, though in the unsystematic manner of a long historical development, as (1) retributive, (2) disciplinary, (3) probationary and evidential, (4) revelational, (5) sacrificial, (6) eschatological.

IV. The present more systematic approach may begin with the relation of the individual to the society, since this constantly conditions his share of suffering. Selfishness is the supreme failure in life, and "altruism" is as truly an element in our constitution as "egoism", though various causes give "egoism" the predominance. But the group counts historically prior to the individual, and the "discovery" of the individual has been a long and costly process. We can never separate the "rights" of the individual from his obligations, for his "rights" themselves are socially constituted. He is bound to serve others, and all service brings suffering. But "self-sacrifice" is rational, from the social standpoint.

V. One, though not the only one, of the causes of suffering is moral evil, springing from the abuse of human freedom. This may affect body as well as mind, since they constantly interact. Such suffering can be regarded as retributive, for retribution has a true place in a theory of punishment. But adequacy of divine retribution cannot be demonstrated from the course of the present order, nor can death be regarded as the penalty of sin. Speculations as to cosmic evil do not solve the problem of its existence, but simply extend the range of the problem. The moral responsibility of human freedom would be destroyed by a theory of "necessary" evil, whether that of an Adamic Fall, or that of evolution.

VI. Our main problem is how to reconcile the vast amount of suffering not to be explained by moral evil with the goodness of the Creator and Ruler of the world. Here we may usefully divide the problem into three parts, viz., as seen in Nature, in History and in the experience of the individual. Nature's ways are marked by regularity, dynamic movement to some goal and conformity to a corporate structure, and the achievement of these characteristics entails much suffering; but each of them is essential to the good we enjoy. Jesus interpreted Nature as beneficent.

VII. History is largely a record of human suffering, but the factor of human freedom and responsibility must not be forgotten. Features of history that seem to deny the divine control of it are (1) the slowness of progress and the cost of it, (2) the element of "chance" in its course, (3) the triumph of might over right. But we may reject the pessimism of Schopenhauer in favour of the optimism of Jesus if we believe with Him that the temporal order serves an eternal purpose.

VIII. The problem becomes practical and acute in the individual experience. But before we deny the reality of divine providence, we should recognize that personal relation to God lifts the problem to a new level, on which there is a new standard of values and the operation of a larger purpose. On this level, there is a transvaluation of suffering. But a great residual problem remains, and our only hope of facing this successfully is by appeal to the love of God, who does not shrink from suffering, in us, and with us, and for us.

IX. The claim that God suffers rests on the Biblical revelation of Him and particularly on the fact of the suffering of Jesus Christ. But the Greek theology of the Early Church, on philosophical grounds, rejected any ascription of suffering to God. Modern theology has largely returned to the assertion of divine passibility. But there are serious philosophical objections which must be faced, viz., that divine passibility implies (1) frustration, (2) entanglement in the time-process, (3) the conception of a God less than the Absolute of philosophy. These objections, however, can be met, for (1) self-limitation is not frustration, (2) God is not in time, but time is in God, (3) the concept of the Absolute must not oust that of the God and Father of Jesus Christ, continuously active in creation and redemption. Has God's love any meaning, if it is not costly to Him, as well as to Jesus? Both the suffering of the Son and the suffering of the Holy Spirit reveal and imply a suffering Father.

X. How does such divine suffering "redeem"? It is a fact of experience that men are reconciled to God by the Cross of Christ; how far can we explain this? We can say that the actuality of our sin (i.e., its realization in history) concerns God, and that sin will always bring suffering, not only to the sinner, but to the Holy God. The free acceptance of this suffering by God is one aspect of His grace. This is visible in our human history through the Cross of Christ, in which we see as much of the suffering God as is possible for man. The classical theories rightly assert, in their various "metaphors", the objectivity of the divine suffering. The common truth that underlies them is the objective transformation of the consequences of man's sin into the occasion of God's grace, a transformation historically achieved on Calvary, as the projection into time of eternal reality.

XI. The fellowship of God with man which has its earthly centre at the Cross has two great applications to the residual problem of unexplained human suffering. Man can the more firmly trust God because of His actualized "sympathy", and man is invited to share in the fellowship of Christ's sufferings, by which evil is transformed to good. Thus the redemptive work of Christ is continued in all who are His, and the eternal reality is continually being actualized in the temporal world.

XII. We may translate the argument into the practical motto of *Solvitur Patiendo* for the life of Christian faith. Suffering must be interpreted from within the creative fellowship with God through Christ. This enables the believer to welcome even suffering as divinely given opportunity. Through suffering, we learn both humility and sympathy with others and we have the opportunity to give effective witness to our faith. Fellowship with Jesus implies "cross-bearing" with Him. The conditions of such a *Solvitur Patiendo* are (1) a persistent purpose, (2) a reference to something beyond the suffering, (3) the winning of peace *through* suffering, and not by evasion of it.

SUFFERING
HUMAN AND DIVINE

CHAPTER I

THE FACT OF SUFFERING

THE greatest play of the greatest dramatist centres in the subject of this book. Shakespeare's "King Lear" is supremely a study of human suffering, though that suffering opens out upon many other aspects of life. What can it suggest to us? In approaching the theme through the tragedy, we borrow the incomparable insight of the dramatist into human life. We get the inner point of view as his mind conceives it and his art reconstructs it, we get his "emotion recollected in tranquillity".

Three truths at least about human suffering will be impressed upon us by the thoughtful reading of this play. They impress us the more because they are not presented in didactic form, but with the resources of great art. They are not entangled with any theory about life, any moralization concerning life, any theological or philosophical doctrine by which life has to be interpreted. They are simply the truth about man's life as seen in "Shakespeare's cloudless, boundless, human view". The first of them is that the mental or

spiritual factors in human suffering are far more intense in their operation than the physical. Think of
the storm upon the heath, when the outer conditions
of Nature parallel and illustrate the inner and spiritual
storm raging within these human personalities. We are
meant to realize that the worst that Nature can do is
negligible as compared with the suffering of the storm
within:—

> "the tempest in my mind
> Doth from my senses take all feeling else
> Save what breaks there."

The physical suffering is real, but by comparison with
the spiritual it is less than nothing, for Lear even wel-
comes it:—

> "This tempest will not give me leave to ponder
> On things would hurt me more."

Physical pain can be an invited anodyne when spiritual suffering becomes intense. The test of memory is
for all of us significant. I know a father whose little
boy had to undergo a slight but painful operation in
which an anaesthetic could not be used. The father remembers the child's cries to him for help against the
surgeon as the most agonizing moment of his own life
—yet the child, now a man, has completely forgotten
the incident. The term "suffering" is apt to suggest

the picture of a hospital with its wards and operating theatre; yet beyond the visible fact of physical pain there may be the hidden suffering of frustrated plans, wearing anxieties, and the dread of what is yet to come, often harder to bear than the actual pain.

The second point to notice is the close inter-relation of suffering and moral evil. That Shakespeare is no moralizer is sufficiently indicated by the way in which he penalizes moralizing and tedious *dramatis personae*, such as Malvolio. But he does bring out, in this play as in so many others, the truth that the evil act has evil consequences. We may think of the way in which Lear's foolish egoism and Gloucester's unbridled lust bring in their train much physical and spiritual suffering. As Edgar puts it:—

> "The gods are just, and of our pleasant vices
> Make instruments to plague us."

Whatever we make of it, both the course of individual life and the social order to which we belong have this much of "morality" in their very texture—that the evil act somehow and for someone brings evil consequences. We cannot evade the force of this fact by saying that it is no more than a trick of definition, and that we agree to call "evil" those things which have evil consequences. The partial truth which gives plausibility to the evasion is that morality is worked out slowly in a social setting by trial and error, and that the moral sanction does evolve in closest relation to the pressure of the society upon the individual. But the history of the *origins* of human morality is one thing, and the question of its ultimate *source* is quite another. Plain and honest men would agree that some part of the great harvest of suffering springs from roots they would call evil, such as man's inhumanity to man. We must not try to generalize the truth, as did the friends of Job, and link up all suffering with moral evil; but neither must we ignore their connection. The actual distribution of the suffering incurred may often seem to us unjust, but that raises questions which will meet us later. There is an instinctive feeling in most of us that evil ought not to "get away with it" without suffering, and the experience of life does often confirm us in that demand. "Crime does not pay", as the criminal himself will frequently admit. Even when the evil man keeps visible success within his grasp, there may be, as Eliphaz puts it, "a sound of terrors in his ears".[1]

The third contribution which the discerning reader finds in the drama is its rebuke of sheer pessimism. In spite of all the ingratitude and treachery and fiendish cruelty, there are qualities of piety and loyalty and pity which are thrown the more into prominence by

[1] Job XV. 21.

their dark background. Cordelia's unbroken love for
the father who has so deeply wronged her would not
be what it is without the wrong. In King Lear himself, and to some extent in Gloucester, we watch that
growth in character which comes only through the
experience of suffering. By that very suffering, Lear
is moved to say:—

> "Poor naked wretches, whereso'er you are,
>   That bide the pelting of this pitiless storm,
>   How shall your houseless heads and unfed sides,
>   Your loop'd and window'd raggedness, defend you
>   From seasons such as these? O, I have ta'en
>   Too little care of this!"

A world in which such sympathy can be evoked is not
a hopeless world. If it be said that the tragic conclusion, the deaths of Lear and Cordelia at the moment
of their reconciliation, simply exaggerates the suffering and accentuates the tragedy of human life, our
answer must be given in terms of Bradley's fine judgment:—"The heroic being, though in one sense and
outwardly he has failed, is yet in another sense supe-
rior to the world in which he appears . . . an idea
which, if developed, would transform the tragic view
of things. It implies that the tragic world, if taken
as it is presented, with all its error, guilt, failure, woe
and waste, is no final reality, but only a part of reality taken for the whole, and when so taken, illusive;

and that if we could see the whole, and the tragic facts in their true place in it, we should find them, not abolished, of course, but so transmuted that they had ceased to be strictly tragic." [2]

From this glance at a great work of art, we have gained the suggestions that spiritual suffering is a more important part of our problem than physical pain, that the problem of suffering is intimately bound up with that of moral evil, and that a transformation of the meaning of suffering can radically alter our judgment of its place in the universe. All three truths will be prominent in what follows, but we may best begin with some consideration of the "bare fact" of suffering—though, strictly speaking, there can never be a "bare fact" in the consciousness of a spiritual being, who always adds his own interpretation, even in the mere perception of it.

The capacity for suffering belongs to our physical nature from birth to death. The perils of disease and accident lurk in ambush for even the healthiest man or woman. The popularization of science has made most of us microbe-conscious. The occasional epidemic which breaks through our elaborate precautions reminds us from time to time of our vulnerability.

[2] A. C. Bradley, *Shakespearean Tragedy*, p. 324. This view should be carefully distinguished from the theory noticed in the next chapter, that suffering itself is unreal. Nor is Bradley thinking of a merely æsthetic contrast (cf. J. S. Whale, *The Problem of Evil*, p. 23).

The toll of the road that passes our doors brings home to us something of the meaning of the daily tale of accident on sea and land, in the air and under the earth. "Air Raid Precautions" have awakened even the feeblest imagination to the sense of new perils, and the bombing of some distant city no longer seems far away. The degradation and expulsion from home and country of so many thousands of our fellow-men has shocked the conscience of the Western world. We are less likely to-day to sing of "old, unhappy, far-off things, and battles long ago", for the daily newspaper supplies more than enough of their modern parallels. The very knowledge of these things and its rapid diffusion has greatly increased our unrest and has largely contributed to the sense of nervous strain under which so many are living to-day.

Our conscious reaction to all this mass of physical suffering reminds us on the large scale of what we all know on the smaller one of our own lives—that physical pain acquires new intensity for a self-conscious being. Beyond all this actuality or possibility of physical suffering, there is the immense extension of it which springs from the very constitution of the human consciousness. Even when perfect health of body is enjoyed, there can be the haunting fear of its loss, especially as we grow older and contemplate the possibility of long and wearisome dependence on others. We look before and after; we suffer spiritually through bitter memories or anxious forebodings. We know the sense of personal frustration, the shame of folly and of moral evil, the many reverberations of personal suffering which arise from our social relations. There can be no doubt whatever that our capacity for suffering is enormously increased by the spirituality of our nature.

These are some of the things which we must face frankly, if we are ever to face them fearlessly. It is futile to try to forget them, and in the modern world it is increasingly difficult and dangerous to attempt this. We must not dwell on them as if they were the whole of life, and turn them into a morbid obsession. But neither must we try to force them prematurely into the conventional categories, moral or religious. The first condition of strength is truth—truth to the facts of life. "A fact is too sacred a thing to be sacrificed on the altar of any generalization." There is positive value in any contact with the sheer realities of life, before we begin to interpret them. Such was the contact made by King Lear, finding expression in words of which the sanity stands out the more against the background of his madness. He is contrasting the unreal past, when he was surrounded by flattering courtiers, with the stark realities of the storm-swept heath:—

"To say *ay* and *no* to everything that I said! *Ay* and *no* too was no good divinity. When the rain came to wet me once, and the wind to make me chatter; when the thunder would not peace at my bidding, there I found 'em, there I smelt 'em out. Go to, they are not men of their words; they told me I was everything; 'tis a lie;—I am not ague-proof."

There is the stubborn fact, spiritual as well as physical, because taken up into a human self-consciousness, "I am not ague-proof".

It is salutary, if sometimes overwhelming, to discover that the wind and the rain care nothing for human comfort, and show no trace of moral responsibility. The great inevitabilities of nature mass their clouds and roll their thunder against us, not only as though there were no God, but as though there were no man. To men of our half-belief, this is apt to be even more terrifying. Shakespeare's play has shown us human lives in the grip of such inevitabilities, natural and spiritual. The onward sweep of circumstance was as remorseless as the storm on the heath beating on the shelterless fugitives. In both realms, though more clearly in Nature's, we have the chance to learn the fundamental lesson of the lowest class in God's school—that God is greater than man. Nature claims us, and as some of us still believe, Nature is God's. As long as we have bodies we shall belong to Nature's

9

order, and the order of Nature is part of the revelation of God's ways with man. We are surely wrong when we set grace in sharp antithesis to Nature. In the awe-inspiring resistlessness of the natural forces—storm and sea, earthquake and volcano, the rush of the river in flood and the unceasing motion of the planets—the believer in a Creator will hear His voice and accept the partial revelation of Himself. Whatever our life means, it is something to be worked out amid the clash of material forces, which show no apparent regard for it. We may refuse, and we shall rightly refuse, to regard our interests in life as no more than a child's toy swept along by the flood. But that flood is part of our experience, and must contribute part of its meaning.

Let us change our metaphor, and employ one which has appealed to discerning minds through many generations—that of the loom of life:—

"Under the breath of laughter, deep in the tide of tears,
I hear the Loom of the Weaver that weaves the Web of
    Years".[3]

Goethe has made the whirring loom of time the means by which the Earth-Spirit weaves for God the garment by which we see Him.[4] In the Old Testament,

[3] Alfred Noyes, *The Loom of Years*.
[4] *Faust*, Part I, lines 508, 509.

the flying shuttle of the weaver's loom becomes a type
of the brevity of human life,[5] and Hezekiah, in what
seemed his mortal sickness, compared his finished life
with the web rolled up when cut off from the thrum.[6]
The metaphor is suggestive. It gives us the duality of
experience without distorting it into a dualism. The
unity of the whole is not destroyed by the comings
and goings of the shuttle above and beneath the fixed
threads of the warp. Within each of us there is a little
world of his own, swept with confused alarms of
struggle and flight, a world of instincts and passions,
dim forebodings and frenzied desires, petty triumphs
and shameful defeats, an inner world which finds expression in the real, but limited freedom of our will.
In the pattern of the whole, for good or for evil, the
two worlds are brought into relation, and the ultimate meaning of life lies in that relation. It is useless
for the shuttle to quarrel with the disposition of the
threads of the warp. It is as foolish to deny their existence as it is to think of ourselves as no more than one
of them.

In the poem to which reference has been made,
Hezekiah is represented as saying of his sickness, "it
was for my peace that I had great bitterness". Whether
or not that be true of any man will depend on his

[5] Job VII. 6.
[6] Isaiah XXXVIII. 12.

personal reaction to the suffering. What is our first reaction to some physical pain from which there is no escape? Probably, to "grin and bear it", the grin being our tribute to that social order to which we belong. We must keep up appearances, and make as light as we can of the suffering—whether because of our own pride, or because we want to save others from suffering sympathetically with us. I am not thinking of another type of reaction, which plays for sympathy, since that belongs rather to the "Malade Imaginaire", whereas Molière, acting the part in spite of intense pain, before he hurried off the stage to die, shows us the genuine reaction of the brave man in such a social order as ours. When the pain passes beyond a certain point, the sufferer identifies himself with it; he is that pain and nothing else.[7] Of course, if he has some vital faith in God that is more than conventional, his reaction will include some attempt to submit to the will of God, or rather, some attempt to accept the suffering as the will of God. If he has no such faith, it will just seem to him "bad luck", with no more to be said about it. Whether the consciousness that suffering is the common lot brings any alleviation is open to dispute, and widely different views seem to be held. On the one hand it is claimed:—

[7] Cf. Aldous Huxley, *Ends and Means*, p. 233.

"That loss is common would not make
My own less bitter, rather more".[8]

On the other hand, it is said that "there is no reflexion which more substantially relieves the pressure of actual distress".[9] The truth seems to lie with the latter view. In discovering that *"Humanum est pati"*, we get deeper down to the heart of life than when we discover that *"Humanum est errare"*, however important be that lesson also. We are made to feel a certain kinship with other men, which means a larger potentiality of life, through the very experience of suffering with them.

But there is a deeper discovery even than this, to be made through the experience of suffering. It has been most forcibly expressed, not by any theologian, but by one of our contemporary novelists.[10] He is describing one who had no religion, and felt no need of it. To her came the shock of a great bereavement, and then, later, the suffering of incurable pain:—"Beneath all the gaiety, the zest, the joy of life, she had, unknown to herself, been carrying about in her this tremendous capacity for suffering and had never suspected it. . . . The thrill of pain had seemed to carry a message. . . . Somehow she had seemed to feel God

[8] Tennyson, *In Memoriam* (VI).
[9] W. E. Hocking, *The Meaning of God in Human Experience*, p. 200.
[10] Robert Hichens, in *Mrs. Marden* (1919), pp. 44, 236, 237.

in it. The thrill of it had been like an assertion: "You belong to me and you cannot escape me." . . . The thrust of pain through her body had been also like a thrust of mysterious knowledge through her soul." I think that does represent a real and vital line of discovery, all the more impressive because it springs from the "bare fact" of suffering, as yet unentangled with any theory about God and His ways with man. It is the discovery that we belong to Someone bigger than ourselves, the discovery of the truth which has been emphasized in this chapter, that Nature is God's, and that Nature reveals God in some of His inevitabilities.

Even so, pain is an evil, against which we instinctively protest, from which we instinctively struggle to escape, and against which we wage war by every means that our civilization offers. Whether it is to be more than an evil, whether it can be transformed into a good, for ourselves, for the human race, or for God, will depend upon our own attitude towards it. We saw that the mental factor in human suffering enormously increases its range, and puts it incomparably beyond the suffering of the animal world. But here, as so often, the possibility of evil carries with it the possibility of good. Our spiritual nature equips us with an instrument of unlimited power—the power to transform the meaning of suffering. The classical expression of this is to be found in Wordsworth's "Character of the Happy Warrior", in familiar words which can hardly be quoted too often:—

"Who, doomed to go in company with Pain,
And Fear, and Bloodshed, miserable train!
Turns his necessity to glorious gain;
In face of these doth exercise a power
Which is our human nature's highest dower;
Controls them and subdues, transmutes, bereaves
Of their bad influence, and their good receives."

CHAPTER II

SOME EXPLANATIONS OF SUFFERING

A THEOLOGICAL student, after a long time spent as a patient in hospital, told me that he entered it expecting to get a good many "points for preaching" out of his experience. As a matter of fact, however, he found that the dulling effect of suffering was too much for him; his mind was not alert enough to profit by the experience. That would probably be true for most of us, especially when the suffering is sufficiently intense to make us identify ourselves with it, to the exclusion of everything else. Only when we see it in retrospect can it be made to yield its tribute. But by that time the vividness of the impressions is lost; we are now contemplating something that is in part an abstraction from the concrete experience. We are liable to "the psychologist's fallacy" applied to ourselves; we read back into a former experience that which is true only of our later reflection on it. One of the reasons, in fact, why the meaning of life is so elusive is that we can usually reflect only on the memory of an experience, and not on the experience itself.

On the other hand, our general attitude towards the problem of suffering, the kind of explanation we habitually give of it whilst we are detached spectators, will undoubtedly condition our actual bearing of physical pain and mental suffering. The selfish and querulous spirit displayed by some sufferers is much more their own fault than they would be willing to admit. It is their own fault because they have not prepared themselves in advance for what is the common lot of men. The effective reactions to life must usually be more or less automatic. Whether it be driving a motor-car, or playing a violin, or bearing pain, it is the discipline of previous training which counts in the moment of necessary decision, in which conscious reflection can have little or no place. Even the ritual of worship, for those who elaborate this side of religion, is said to yield its most spiritual results only when it has become automatic, and the mind is set free for that which lies beyond and above the ritual acts.

Our habitual explanation of suffering, the place it holds in our general interpretation of life, our moral reaction to it, our religious faith, is therefore of practical importance to us. Our explanation may break down, or call for revision, under the practical test, but, whatever it is, it will count for something. Just as our capacity to understand the world of Nature will depend on what interpretative principles we bring to the task, so is it with the particular part of our experience which is called "suffering". The well-equipped physicist, chemist or biologist sees far more in any phenomenon than the ordinary man, just because of what he brings to it. In no smaller measure suffering will yield its secret only to those who can lift it into some larger setting.

As we review some of the current and typical explanations of the fact of suffering, it is important to recognize that they belong to different levels, and that each is relevant only on the particular level to which it belongs. Thus it is possible and useful to consider pain simply as a biological or psychological fact, springing from our physical and mental nature. On a higher level, it becomes part of the experience of a moral being, for whom it may be explained as the necessary discipline of development, or as the opportunity to bear social witness to the virtue of resolute endurance. Finally, at the highest level, that of religion, suffering has often been transmuted into sacrifice, and been made an offering to God. The variety of possible explanations suggests that none of them will cover the whole field, or be applicable to every instance of suffering. The relevancy will depend on the particular "level of discourse", the degree of development in the sufferer's own attitude.

At this point, a warning may not be out of place.

EXPLANATIONS OF SUFFERING

A distinguished missionary in China [1] has told us of his encounter with the evangelist of a native sect, busy in denouncing the Christian religion as cruel and inhuman. When challenged to prove his charge, he produced a book by a medical missionary, in which there were anatomical and surgical illustrations:—"Ignorant of the humane object of surgery, he regarded operations as proof of the cruelty of Christians." Less crudely, but not less wrongly, we may misjudge a universe in which we have not yet climbed high enough to get a large view of things.

On the biological level, the most obvious interpretation of physical pain is as Nature's danger-signal. The healthy functioning of an organ or an organism seems always to be accompanied by the feeling of pleasure, or at least of contentment; pain is the warning that something is wrong, and is so far beneficent. Our reactions to pain have their own particular physiological receptors. Pain is not due, as is often supposed, to the excessive stimulation of a sensory nerve, but to definite pain-spots, with their net-work of nerve-fibres. Just as the skin has special organs for the sensations of warmth, cold and touch, so it has for pain. Thus, "when a sharp point is pressed on the skin the sensation becomes painful just before the pressure is

[1] Timothy Richard, *Forty-five Years in China* (1916), p. 89f.

19

sufficient to cause penetration." [2] To low grades of stimuli these pain-spots are not responsive, but when the danger-point is reached, when, for example, pleasant warmth becomes destructive heat, the pain-spot comes into operation. Nature has evolved these danger-signals to act like the fuse-wire of an electrical system, and if we admit purposive evolution at all, we may surely see it here. For the preservation of the individual and for the development of the race, pain is essential. It is worth noticing that physiology offers an interesting parallel to spiritual or moral atrophy. Disease may abolish pain without affecting the sense of touch, just as a hardened conscience may gradually lose its sense of guilt.

The "instinctive" appetites, which are the fundamental driving forces of life, animal and human, involve some sort of uneasy sensation,[3] from which escape is sought through the satisfaction of the appetite. Broadly speaking, it seems to be the avoidance of pain, rather than the pursuit of pleasure, which urges us forward, and ministers to the continuance and evolution of the race. This must not be taken to mean that "pain is the necessary background of pleasure",

[2] Starling, *Principles of Human Physiology*, ed. 7, p. 434, on which book the statements of the above paragraph are chiefly based. Drawings of the four types of "touch" organs can be seen in *The Science of Life*, by H. G. Wells, Julian Huxley and G. P. Wells, p. 101.

[3] James Ward, *Psychological Principles* (1920), p. 279.

since there may be the contrast between a lesser and a greater pleasure as a sufficient motive for action.[4] Both pain and pleasure may be regarded as springing from the neutral and common ground of "contentment".[5] But the intenser quality of pain makes it an important factor in the awakening of self-consciousness. That which I feel so intensely as *mine* undeniably asserts the existence of *me*. Pleasure is probably not so influential a factor, except at moments of marked intensity, just because we can accept it more passively, whereas pain urges us to assert ourselves in the escape from it. As the biologist will tell us, "It is only when organisms must struggle against heavy odds to gain comfort that they succeed in bettering themselves." [6] Only when the sensation of pain is taken up into some dominant purpose which transforms it, will the fear of pain be overcome, as it is in the martyr who deliberately thrusts his hand into the flames. Pain in itself is "something to be avoided",[7] and the abnormal attraction it exercises in masochism and some forms of asceticism has other explanations and need not concern us here.

Biology can teach us that no interpretation of suffering is justifiable which takes account only of the

[4] Tennant, *Philosophical Theology*, II, p. 198.
[5] Ward, *op. cit.*, p. 278.
[6] J. H. Bradley, *Parade of the Living* (1931), p. 251.
[7] W. McDougall, *An Outline of Psychology* (1923), p. 268.

individual. For better, for worse, we are what we are through our membership of a social order, past, present and future. We are in debt to that social order for much of our good; there is nothing unjust in the demand of Nature that we should repay that debt. Before any issue of morality or religion is raised, and on the purely biological level, it is common sense to start our thinking with the fact that all life is conditioned just as much socially as individually. This is an elementary observation; yet how much of our complaint and resentment springs from the selfish claim to be somehow exempt from the common lot, somehow privileged to receive and not to give! If it be said that the sting of much human suffering lies in its apparent futility, its utter inability to contribute anything to the good of others, the answer must spring from such interpretation of suffering on a higher level as will show that the futility may be far less than it seems.

Certainly, new possibilities emerge when we rise from the purely "natural" to the moral level of interpretation. So far as we agree to value courage, endurance, patience, sympathy and a host of other virtues, we are bound to recognize that suffering, or the capacity for it, is their necessary condition. Character depends on volition, and volition must face risks and encounter suffering in order to have any real value for character-building. The man who engages in the hardier sports joyfully accepts such risks and endures such hardships for the game's sake. The father who shelters his son from all risks of suffering will probably ruin his character; there is a sound principle in the historic words of Edward III at the battle of Creçy, when urged to send aid to his hard-pressed son —"Let the boy win his spurs". Obviously, there are definite limits to the application of the principle, though it may be extraordinarily difficult to know just where to draw them. It will not explain the long drawn-out continuance of suffering through some incurable disease, so far as the present world is concerned; there is no opportunity in this life for the exercise of the character that may be achieved through the suffering. The principle of moral development does not answer Cowper's question, "Why was existence given to a creature that might possibly, and would probably, become wretched in the degree that I have been so?" [8] It does not explain the cutting short of some young life full of bright promise, and the shadow of a great bereavement that rests on others for all the years to come.

On the other hand, we must not overlook the possibility that other principles may operate, where that of moral discipline through suffering fails to explain

[8] *William Cowper*, by H. L'Anson Fausset, p. 310.

its mystery. Some sufferers have been able to exercise an extraordinary influence on those who ministered to them. Every minister could tell of someone he has known in his pastoral work whose gracious personality has made the sick-bed a centre of influence for good perhaps greater than any service which could have been rendered in health. It would be difficult to disentangle a poet's achievement from the temperament which made him vulnerable beyond other men. A great and crushing bereavement can be the inspiration to social service, which might not otherwise have been rendered. There is a striking example of this in the life of John Bright. When his young wife was lying dead in the house, he was visited by his friend, Richard Cobden, who said to him, "There are thousands of houses in England at this moment where wives, mothers and children are dying of hunger. Now, when the first paroxysm of your grief is past, I would advise you to come with me, and we will never rest till the Corn Law is repealed." So began their historic co-operation.[9] Such an example warns us against the self-absorption of grief, which may easily become a subtle form of selfishness.

It is when we rise to the level of religion that we meet both our greatest difficulties and the most inspiring suggestions in regard to human suffering. Our

[9] *Life of Richard Cobden*, by J. Morley (1903), p. 190.

greatest difficulties—for the very existence of suffering in its unimaginable amplitude and intensity is the most serious of all challenges to theism. Moral evil is much more easily explained, as due to the abuse of moral freedom. But there is an overwhelming irrationality in the apparent distribution of suffering, as well as its amount, which has often given rise to the dilemma—either God is not benevolent or God is not omnipotent. Probably more people lose faith in God through what seems to them the maladjustment of Providence than through any other cause.

On the other hand, the level of our greatest difficulties is also that of the highest resources with which to meet them. It is only when suffering is brought into relation with God that its larger significance can be seen. More especially, as will be argued here, it is the suffering of God Himself, revealed through Jesus Christ, which throws most light on the suffering of man, and bestows most strength on the sufferer.

Before, however, we turn to the Bible, for what it has to say about human suffering, we may glance at some contrasting attempts to deal with it, in the light of a large or cosmic setting. All philosophies and all religions have to meet the challenge of suffering, but we must confine our attention here to three distinct types of approach, viz., those of Buddhism, Stoicism and Christian Science.

Everyone is familiar with the striking story of Prince Gautama's renunciation of his high estate, through his deep sympathy with the sufferings of mankind. The spectacle of decrepit old age, of disease, and of death moved him to seek the retirement in which he might find the right way of escape from the miseries of life. After study and protracted ascetism had failed him, the great illumination came through a new attitude towards the self. The doctrine of "dependent origination" at which he finally arrived taught that suffering depends on our attachment to existence, and is inextricably linked with our desire to exist. The right remedy lies in the extirpation of this desire from consciousness, and this can be attained only by the denial of self, both in practice and in theory. The fundamental illusion is to say, "I am"—a conclusion which stands in sharpest contrast with the typically Western assertion of Descartes, that this is the fundamental certainty. If Christianity be the religion which most exalts personality, Buddhism is that which reduces it to the lowest point—that at which it disappears, so far as theory goes. The Buddhist saint does not suffer, because all suffering belongs to those changes of form which belong to a nonexistent self. However wretched therefore he may be in body, he cannot be wretched in mind, for he knows no sorrow or lamentation, no grief or despair.[10] It should be noticed that this attitude (in its original form) is not a religion at all, but an ethical discipline, which needs no gods and no philosophy beyond this sweeping nihilism. In spite of the noble elements in Buddhism, its denial of personality will prevent any general acceptance of it by the West.

Stoicism followed a very different path. Its ethics were set within a world-order of Universal Law and Reason, working inexorably, and calling for absolute submission to its inexorable course. Within this fixed order, man's wisdom was to live according to his own higher nature, which reflected the outer reason and was part of it. The emotional side of life was unnatural and worthless; the ideal of the wise man was to become impassible, dependent only on himself, and always at liberty to terminate by suicide the suffering which might be too great for him. This self-dependence did not mean a selfish withdrawal from life; on the contrary the common fellowship of men was deduced from the universal reason, and the high ideals of the Stoic sense of duty are familiar to us through the pages of Epictetus and Marcus Aurelius. In many ways Stoic ethics approximated to the Christian, and doubtless influenced them in both theory

10 Warren, *Buddhism in Translations*, p. 422.

and practice. Yet this high and austere fortitude was a philosophy for the spiritual aristocrat, and never possessed that wide sweep of democratic appeal which established Christianity in the Western world. The fact of suffering was too formidable for such guerilla fighting to cope with it. The Christian faith overcame suffering by taking it into its embrace and rejoicing in its possession.

In our times, the cult known as "Christian Science" has attracted a considerable following. In some respects, it stands midway between Buddhism and Stoicism. Like Buddhism, it traces all suffering of body and mind to illusion, though the truth that puts the illusion to flight is the denial not of the self but of all that is material. Like Stoicism, it makes a high demand upon the individual consciousness, though this is reinforced by a theory of relentless idealism, the existence of Spirit and nothing but spirit.[11] The curious history of this new religion and the startling inconsistencies which it seems able to assimilate are set out in H. A. L. Fisher's vigorous and amusing little book, called *Our New Religion,* but with these features of it we are not concerned. It must be sufficient to say that "Christian Science" is not to be reconciled with

[11] A clear and conveniently brief statement of the theory of Christian Science, made by one of its representatives, will be found in the *Encyclopaedia of Religion and Ethics,* III, p. 576-579.

New Testament Christianity, which gives to the Cross a positive and central place and does not regard it as "the last and greatest temptation to believe in the power of evil with which (Jesus) was confronted". The briefest philosophical refutation is that "if evil is illusion, the illusion is an evil".[12]

The element of truth in "Christian Science" is its use of the power of the mind over the body. This truth receives its proper scientific recognition in the modern practice of psycho-therapy. Its central principle is that "the mind is not a complete unity".[13] Beneath the conscious mind, there is the subconscious, "the background which contains all our past memories, our primitive instincts, and deep-seated wishes". The forgotten or misunderstood distortions of these are often responsible for otherwise inexplicable mental suffering and disorder. By various means of enquiry and treatment, the psycho-therapist brings those causes to light and endeavours to remove them. Though the disease and the treatment are primarily mental, and concern functional rather than organic disorder, the inter-relations of the two are properly recognized. Psycho-therapy thus forms a special branch of ordinary medical and surgical work. On the other

[12] Tennant, *Philosophical Theology*, II, p. 181.
[13] W. Brown, *Psychological Methods of Healing* (1938), p. 192. This book gives a clear and balanced account of psycho-therapy, by one of its most distinguished English practitioners.

hand, its relation to religion is fully recognized by some, at least, of its practitioners. Just as the temporary relation of the patient to the psycho-therapist has points of contact with personal faith in religious experience, so the "sublimation" by which primitive instincts etc. are directed to higher ends forms a parallel to, and may be promoted by, religious faith in the fullest sense. Whilst psycho-therapy may be held to provide an alternative explanation of many "religious" miracles of healing, it ought not to be regarded in the least as destructive of the higher truths of religion itself. Mental process is one thing; its philosophical and therefore its religious foundation and framework belong to a higher level of reality. In the realm of the mind, the cosmos in process of creation within, the same truth holds as for the cosmos without; all we can discover of the *modus operandi* should not prejudice in the least our judgment of ultimate reality.

CHAPTER III

THE PROBLEM OF SUFFERING IN THE OLD TESTAMENT

THIS book is a general study of the meaning of suffering as it presents itself to the modern man, and not a history of the doctrines that relate to suffering. Nevertheless, there are special grounds for devoting a chapter to the interpretation of suffering in the Old Testament. In the first place, the ideas of the Old Testament, here as elsewhere, are fundamental to those of the New, in which we have the classical and normative conceptions of the Christian faith. In the second place, the Old Testament gives us the most comprehensive survey of the problem of suffering from the standpoint of theistic religion which can be found anywhere. In the third place, this survey, with many varieties of interpretation, is enshrined in the successive documents of a developing history, and is free from any suspicion of ecclesiastical convention or dogmatic distortion.

The problem was central in the later religion of Israel for the following reasons: (i) The faith of

Israel was directed towards a divine Being, conceived as personal and active, who had created the world and its inhabitants and ruled them in accordance with a persistent purpose. So long as He was regarded as one God among many others (though even then the only God for Israel), the defeat of Israel in battle could find a natural explanation; the god of the Moabites, for example, might exert himself successfully against the people of Yahweh.[1] But when, through the teaching of the great prophets, all other deities became non-existent for the faithful Israelite, the sufferings of the nation demanded some other explanation. Why should Israel suffer, when Israel was the people of Yahweh, and all power was His? (ii) This demand was accentuated, when the order of Yahweh's government of the world was interpreted by these same prophets on moral lines. In earlier days, some national disaster, such as the famine in the time of David, might be traced back to the survival of a blood-feud, which required ritual expiation[2]; only the sacred oracle could decide how Israel had offended the deity. But the prophets replaced the sacred oracle by the tribunal of the moral consciousness; if men did justice and loved mercy and walked humbly before God,[3] they

[1] II Kings III. 27, where the wrath belongs to Chemosh; cf. the Moabite Stone.
[2] II Samuel XXI.
[3] Micah VI. 8.

expected to prosper under His hand, and the failure to do so raised awkward questions. (iii) These questions became more insistent as more regard was paid to the significance of the individual within the group. In the earlier days, the clan or the family was often treated as a unit[4]; but through the religious isolation of Jeremiah and in the explicit teaching of Ezekiel the individual attained more adequate religious and social recognition. This had the result of bringing the problem of suffering to the front, for it was no longer so natural to spread out some misfortune over the misdeeds of a whole group, or even its ancestors; the justice of God must vindicate itself within the course of a single life. (iv) Finally, all this development took place amongst a people without any conception of a *real* life beyond death, which might be used by a just God to compensate for the injustices of this world. Consequently, the problem was felt with all the greater intensity; justice ought to be vindicated here and now as well as in each individual life. The obvious contradictions of experience to this demand created and maintained the problem, inevitably felt by Israel more than by any other people.

As the result, then, of centuries of a very varied history, there emerged certain great principles for the interpretation of human suffering, all of which have

[4] Josh. VII. 24, 25.

some permanent value for our guidance, provided we take them in due proportion and relation. The very fact that there are at least half-a-dozen of these serves to remind us of the complexity of the data and still warns us against too simple an interpretation of them. Suffering is, as we have already seen, one of the universal conditions of life, and our interpretation of suffering must be broad and deep and varied as life itself.

1. The first and most comprehensive of these principles is beyond question the *retributive*. This holds from the time of the great prophets onwards into both Judaism and Christianity. If the government of the world is administered by the one and only God, who is a God of righteousness, then, sooner or later, righteousness on man's part will be rewarded, and unrighteousness punished. In regard to the nation, Amos puts it simply in the words, "Seek good and not evil, that ye may live".[5] The Book of Deuteronomy, which in this respect gathers up the teaching of the eighth century prophets, gives eloquent expression to the principle, notably in the closing exhortation of the thirtieth chapter, which begins, "See, I have set before thee this day life and good, and death and evil". The influence and application of this principle may be

[5] Amos V. 14, cf. III. 6:—"shall evil befall a city, and Yahweh hath not done it?"

seen in the re-writing and editing of the history during the subsequent century, particularly in the framework of "Judges" and "Kings". The principle is
fundamental for much of the Wisdom teaching, and
its most striking literary expression is found in the
Book of Job, where the three friends apply it rigor-
ously to the sufferings of Job. This was the orthodox
doctrine of Israel, and it is carried over, with whatever necessary limitations and modifications, into the
New Testament, where Jesus contrasts the fate of
the obedient and the disobedient by use of the simile
of the house built on either rock or sand.[6] So too the
Apostle Paul, notwithstanding his emphasis on the
doctrine of grace, does not hesitate to say, "we must
all be made manifest before the judgment-seat of
Christ, that each may receive the things done in the
body, according to what he hath done, whether it be
good or bad".[7]

This principle, then, is not to be dismissed as one
that is superseded by the doctrine of divine grace.
The conscience of Israel—and may we not say the
conscience of the world?—requires not only the final
establishment of righteousness in the Kingdom of
God, but also its sufficient vindication in the treatment of individual men. However harsh may seem the

[6] Matt. VII. 24-26.
[7] II Cor. V. 10.

retributive principle when taken alone, and however untrue to our experience of life when made the sole principle for the interpretation of suffering, it remains as much part of the moral order of the universe as does the regularity of Nature, on its lower level. More will be said of this principle in Chapter V dealing with "Suffering and Sin".

2. The retributive principle, starkly severe when taken alone, is frequently relieved in the Old Testament by the complementary principle that suffering can be *disciplinary*, or educational. The wise and devout man is, in fact, entitled to interpret suffering in this way:—

"My son, despise not the chastening of the Lord;
Neither be weary of His reproof." [8]

The word for "chastening" (*musar*) is frequent in the Wisdom-literature, being used of that human discipline by which a father educates his son.[9] Even Eliphaz reminds Job of this, within the general setting of the retributive principle:—

"Happy is the man whom God correcteth:
Therefore despise not thou the chastening of the Almighty." [10]

[8] Prov. III. 11.
[9] Prov. XIII. 24, XV. 5.
[10] Job V. 17, cf. Ps. XCIV. 12.

In the Book of Job, it is, however, Elihu who chiefly brings out the disciplinary value of suffering. He describes at length the sick man, "chastened with pain upon his bed, and with continual strife in his bones",[11] who is brought very near to death in his suffering. But this suffering, interpreted to him by an angelic messenger of God, may move him to the humble penitence which is the condition of recovery, so that finally the sufferer, restored to health, will sing God's praise, saying:—

"I sinned and made crooked that which was straight,
  And it was not requited unto me;
  He redeemed me from passing into the Pit
  And my life looks on the light."

Elihu returns to this, his favourite theme, in a later utterance [12] where we have the contrast of the sinner who will *not* be disciplined into repentance by suffering:—

"The godless in heart lay up anger,
  They cry not when He hath bound them:
  Their soul dies in youth,
  And their life among reprobates."

The two passages together give us as detailed an account of disciplinary suffering and its purpose as we

[11] Job XXXIII. 19 ff.
[12] Job XXXVI. 13 ff.

shall find in the Old Testament, though there are many references to it elsewhere, as experienced by either the nation [13] or the individual.[14] Psalm CVII is a series of miniature paintings describing how the sufferings of the traveller, the prisoner, the sick man and the sailor move them to a prayer that is answered, a petition that culminates in a song of praise. Jonah's selfish grief over the loss of the protecting gourd caricatures the undisciplined soul, unwilling to learn sympathy from suffering. The apocryphal "Wisdom of Solomon" contrasts the disciplinary treatment of Israel with the retributive treatment of the Egyptians:—

"For these, as a father, admonishing them, thou didst prove;
  But those, as a stern king, condemning them, thou didst
    search out." [15]

In the New Testament, the sufferings of Christians are interpreted by the same principle:—"God dealeth with you as with sons",[16] and the useful warning is given:—"All chastening seemeth for the present to be not joyous, but grievous: yet afterward it yieldeth peaceable fruit unto them that have been exercised thereby". The most familiar example of disciplinary

[13] E.g. Hosea X. 10, Jer. VI. 8, X. 24 (LXX), XXX. 11, XXXI. 18; Is. XXVI. 16, Lev. XXVI. 18, 23.
[14] Ps. VI. 1, XXXII. 3-5, CXVIII. 18, CXIX. 67.
[15] Wisdom of Solomon XI. 10.
[16] Heb. XII. 7, cf. Rev. III. 19.

38

suffering is afforded by the experience of the Prodigal Son.[17]

3. A third Old Testament principle is that suffering can be *probationary and evidential*—either to God or man. When the prophet Habakkuk looks out from his watch-tower [18] upon the contemporary world, he sees, much as we can see to-day, violence and oppression and apparently successful tyranny, and he cries to God:—"Wherefore lookest thou upon them that deal treacherously, and holdest thy peace when the wicked swalloweth up the man that is more righteous than he?" [19] The answer has to be found in patient waiting for the retributive principle to be manifested; this calls for the quality of "faithfulness" in the righteous man: "the just shall live by his faithfulness".[20] Such endurance of suffering both proves the quality of the righteous man and witnesses to the truth for which he stands. (This is not explicitly stated, but here, as elsewhere, it is implied.) Thereby the way is opened to some of the noblest heights of Old Testament devotion, for it makes the devout man independent of any visible confirmation of his faith in the justice of God. So in the fine psalm attached to

[17] Luke XV. 16ff.
[18] Hab. II. 1.
[19] Hab. I. 13.
[20] Hab. II. 4; not "by his faith", as in St Paul's quite different application of the words.

39

the Book of Habakkuk, the singer contemplates the failure of all material means of support from field and tree, from fold and stall:—

> "Yet I will rejoice in the Lord,
> I will joy in the God of my salvation." [21]

This is in the spirit of the close of Psalm LXXIII, deservedly recognized as the high-water mark of Old Testament piety, where the "Nevertheless" [22] of the writer matches the "Yet" of the passage just quoted:—

> "Nevertheless I am continually with thee:
> Thou hast holden my right hand.
> Thou shalt guide me with thy counsel,
> And afterward receive me gloriously. [23]
> Whom have I in heaven but thee?
> And there is none upon earth that I desire beside thee;
> My flesh and my heart faileth:
> But God is the rock of my heart and my portion for ever."

There the spiritual suffering of the psalmist has separated the fine gold of such a faith from the alloy of material support for it. [24] He has been proved in the furnace of affliction which is the privilege, not the penalty, of God's people. [25] The Servant of the Lord

---

[21] Hab. III. 18.

[22] The Hebrew form is the same.

[23] There is no sufficient ground for referring the phrase to life beyond death, though that might seem the logical inference.

[24] Though not to the abandonment of the retributive principle; see verse 18.

[25] Is. XLVIII. 10.

was a martyr-witness by his sufferings.[26] But the most striking example of this principle is afforded by the prologue to the Book of Job. It is not properly realized that the prologue to that book presents witness-bearing through suffering as one of its true interpretations. Job is presented as vindicating disinterested religion, sustaining the honour of God, becoming, in the double sense of the word, a "martyr"—a witness and a witness through suffering. There is no way of demonstrating a conviction more forcibly than by suffering for it. The blood of the martyrs, and not the ink of its theologies, is the seed of the Church. Martyrs in this sense are always in a minority, but they are the most powerful of minorities. James Hinton, in his *Mystery of Pain* is not exaggerating when he says, "The pains of martyrs, or the losses of self-sacrificing devotion, are never classed among the evil things of the world. They are its bright places rather, the culminating points at which humanity has displayed its true glory, and reached its perfect level. . . . Conceive all martyrdoms blotted out from the world's history; how blank and barren were the page!" [27] Francis of Assisi, when journeying with a disciple, hungry and wet and numbed with cold, bade him imagine that when they reached their hoped-for shelter, they should

[26] Is. L. 6.
[27] P. 11.

41

be driven from it with insults and blows. To suffer that in patience for the love of Christ would, he said, be perfect joy.[28] As Ugo Bassi says, in Mrs Hamilton King's poem, "The Disciples":—

> "Here and here alone
> Is given thee to suffer for God's sake."

4. A fourth principle, which may be called *revelational,* is implicit, rather than explicit, for it involves a point of view that is modern, rather than ancient. By this principle is meant the way in which suffering enables the prophetic consciousness to enter into a deeper knowledge of God and of His relation to man. The prophet Hosea is the most striking example of this. The tragedy of his own domestic life, which he felt so keenly, colours his whole presentation of the truth concerning God. The older naturalistic idea of the marriage of a god to his land, the people being the progeny, is lifted to a new level and becomes the vehicle of profoundly spiritual conceptions of the relation of God to Israel. As every reader of the Book of Hosea knows, these cover not only the disloyalty of Israel to her divine Husband, but the evangelical confidence that the patient and much-suffering love of God will win her back to that sincere penitence, which is expressed in the closing chapter of the book.

[28] *The Little Flowers,* ed. of 1903, p. 28.

So advanced an idea of God would be inconceivable at that stage of the history, if it were not for the context of Hosea's personal experience, through which God was revealed to him.

Another example of this "revelational" quality in suffering comes to us from the prophet who most closely resembles Hosea in temperament and most clearly shows his influence, viz., Jeremiah. The long story of his sufferings, physical as well as spiritual, cannot here be traced,[29] but they sprang from, or were intensified by the fact of his religious isolation from his contemporaries. Isolation from men threw him the more upon God, and issued in a new type of personal religion, with far-reaching consequences, as we can see from many subsequent Psalms. It is deeply significant that some of the contemporaries of Jesus should have seen in Him the return of Jeremiah [30] and the words in which Jeremiah speaks of himself as "a lamb that is led to the slaughter" were echoed in the great song of the Suffering Servant, and also in the apocalyptic vision of the adoration of the Lamb of God, "who taketh away the sin of the world".[31]

5. It is the Song of the Servant which uniquely illustrates the *sacrificial* principle as applied to the

[29] As they are in my little book, *The Cross of Jeremiah* (1925) or in the fine work of J. Skinner, *Prophecy and Religion* (1922).
[30] Matt. XVI. 14.
[31] Jer. XI. 19, cf. Is. LIII. 7, Rev. V. 6, John I. 29, I Pet. I. 19.

interpretation of human suffering. Israel had received of the Lord's hand double for all her sins [32]; so, from that overplus of suffering, the prophet of the exile fashions the noblest crown for the head of Jesus which the Old Testament can offer, an unconscious fore-shadowing of the crown of thorns. The sufferings of Israel in exile are interpreted as a guilt-offering for the nations of the world, which will not only move them to repentance, but also make for them a sacrificial means of approach to God. They have misinterpreted the sufferings of Israel as the penalty inflicted for Israel's sins; but the death of the nation is to be followed by its glorious resurrection, in the light of which the true meaning of the suffering will be apparent.

Sacrifice as an offering made in worship is not to be identified with suffering, still less with penal suffering. The sacrifices of the Old Testament are rather of the nature of gifts, with more or less of special intention. There is no emphasis on the necessary suffering of the victim, where it is an animal. This suffering is merely the means to an end, viz., that of handing over the gift to the deity on his altar. There is no thought of penal substitution in the sacrifices of the Old Testament. On the other hand, the interpretation of human suffering as a vicarious offering to God

[32] Is. XL. 2.

is definitely reached in the conception of the Suffering Servant in Isaiah LIII.

In the light of this passage, beyond all others, the first Christian preachers explained the sufferings of the Cross of Christ, and they were therein following the suggestions of their Master. Even from a purely human standpoint, the death of Jesus on the Cross was the costliest offering which could be made to God. So Jesus Himself seems to have conceived it—under the figure of a ransom or of a covenant-sacrifice like that of Sinai. Let us remember that all such terms are necessarily figurative, whatever reality they represent. To say that the suffering of Jesus was sacrificial is a quite different thing from saying that it was penal. The idea of penal retribution belongs to a different order of thought, as we have already seen. St Paul employed the penal conception as well as the sacrificial, but Jesus and the first preachers of the Gospel apparently did not. To say that "Christ died for our sins according to the Scriptures" is not necessarily to interpret His suffering as penal.

How far has the figure of sacrifice, as applied to human suffering, any permanent value for ourselves, to whom literal sacrifices are an anachronism? Only in the sense that the suffering of a life, carried on to the supreme point of death, is the costliest gift that can be made to God. It is the Godward side of what, on

the human side, is the witness-bearing of martyrdom.
It has positive value for God, if we conceive that
human personality devoted to His will is the supreme
worth of the world to Him. Just as we can think of
the whole process of creative evolution as having been
shaped by Him to produce such personality, so we
may conceive the utter devotion of such personality
in sacrificial suffering as the fruition of His purpose
in that personality.

6. Finally, we have the *eschatological* principle,
by which the intensity of national suffering is held to
measure the nearness of the deliverance from it—the
belief, in fact, that the night is darkest before the
dawn. The greater part of the literature inspired by this
belief lies outside the Old Testament, but Is. XXIV-
XXVII and the Book of Daniel sufficiently illustrate
the general principle. In the latter, the religious persecution that provoked the Maccabean rebellion is
regarded as the beginning of the end, the coming of
the kingdom of the true Israel [33] to be established by
God. In both the apocalypses which have been named
we note the introduction of angelic powers, [34] good or
evil, as concerned with earthly affairs and involved
in earthly fortunes. In both, also, we find the first
beginnings of a doctrine of resurrection, [35] which was

[33] Dan. VII. 13, cf. verse 27.
[34] Is. XXIV. 21, 22, Dan. X. 13, etc.
[35] Is. XXVI. 19, Dan. XII. 2.

46

to be so important when generalized by the later religions of Judaism, Christianity and Islam. The Hebrew form of belief in a resurrection, based on the
psychology which made the body the essential element
of personality, is to be clearly distinguished from the
Greek doctrine of immortality for which the soul was
all that mattered. This Greek doctrine ultimately influenced the Hellenistic forms of Judaism, as we may
see from the "Wisdom of Solomon". The well-known
passage,[36] which so often to-day claims a place in our
burial services, may be quoted here, because it aptly
resumes some of the Old Testament principles of the
interpretation of suffering:—

"The souls of the righteous are in the hand of God,
  And no torment shall touch them.
 In the eyes of the foolish they seemed to have died;
 And their departure was accounted to be their hurt,
 And their journeying away from us to be their ruin:
 But they are in peace.
 For even if in the sight of men they be punished,
 Their hope is full of immortality;
 And having borne a little chastening, they shall receive
    great good;
 Because God made trial of them and found them worthy
    of Himself.
 As gold in the furnace He proved them
 And as a whole burnt offering He accepted them."

[36] III. 1-6.

As we review these various attempts to interpret the meaning of human suffering, we see that they are all partial, and inadequate to bear the full burden of the mystery even when taken together. But all of them illustrate the power of personal trust in God to carry that burden, unexplained as it might be. In this way, they confirm the general argument of this book —that we cannot meet the challenge of suffering by reason alone, but only by some form of religious faith, which lifts it to a higher level. There is only one exception to the optimism of the Old Testament, and that is to be found in the pessimism of Ecclesiastes. For the writer of that book, God indeed remains, but not the living God of Israel, in whom His people can trust. The world becomes a dreary treadmill, from which the wise man will snatch such respite as he can; there is no evidence of retribution here and no life beyond the grave. The book is an admirable foil, to bring out the brilliance of that triumphant trust in God, notwithstanding all the suffering of man, which is one of the chief glories of the Old Testament.

CHAPTER IV

THE INDIVIDUAL AND THE SOCIETY

"I AM killing myself because I have never sincerely loved any human being all my life. I have accepted kindness and friendship and even love without gratitude and given nothing in return." So ran the letter found on the body of a young woman writer. In the newspaper report of the inquest,[1] it was followed immediately by the sentence, "The Coroner recorded a verdict of 'Suicide while of unsound mind' ". I read that conventional verdict with something of a shock, for surely no more rational statement of the failure of life was ever given. If it be true, as Browning says,[2] that

> "life with all it yields of joy and woe,
> And hope and fear,—believe the aged friend,——
> Is just our chance o' the prize of learning love,"

then failure to win that prize is the uttermost failure of all (though to know that it is failure may be already

---

[1] *The Times*, Jan. 10, 1934.
[2] *A Death in the Desert.*

to have moved beyond its doom). It is the same truth that Robert Southwell expressed three centuries earlier, when he said:—"Not where I breathe, but where I love, I live", whilst fifteen centuries earlier still the Apostle Paul wrote:—"If I have not love, I am nothing".

It is plain matter of fact and not mere sentimentality to say that no one can be happy unless his relations with others are satisfying. That fact rests on the actual constitution of human nature. Both the psychology and the ethics of modern times have increasingly recognized that "egoism" is not more fundamental to human life than "altruism". The attempt to derive the social from the selfish instincts and impulses is abandoned by most competent thinkers today, whilst it is freely recognized that self-regarding and other-regarding dispositions are so subtly blended that neither can find its satisfaction without the other. Selfishness is itself a form of moral suicide, which least of any deserves the name of *euthanasia*. Just as we depend on others biologically, for our entrance into life, and sociologically, for the comfort and amenities of civilized life, so in the moral sphere our self-realization demands the social setting without which our very existence and our consciousness of self could hardly arise. It is only by a false abstraction that a man can think of himself out of all relation to other lives, whilst the simplest forms of self-realization as well as the highest moral achievements are wrought out by the flying shuttle of self across the warp of society.

From this standpoint it is intelligible that "selfish-ness"—the attempt to satisfy one part of our nature without regard to the other—will always entail suffering on the selfish person himself as well as on those of his own circle whom his selfishness disregards. No one, indeed, can estimate how large a portion of the world's suffering is due to this elementary disregard of our social nature and its implications, of which we are all in varying degrees guilty. What is the reason for this predominance of "egoism" over "altruism", which is so marked that, in religious phraseology, "sin" is sometimes defined as selfishness? If we try to answer the question on the level of the present chapter (i.e., without regard to religious doctrine and ethics), we shall say something like this—that man is indeed moved by other-regarding as well as by self-regarding instincts, such as sympathy, pity and various kinds of love, but that those instincts lie below the level of consciousness to which "egoism" and "altruism" properly apply. They are natural endowments, part of that equipment of human nature which has its roots in a long line of biological ancestry in the sub-human world. "Natural" behaviour is at this level purely instinctive behaviour. But in man the level of self-consciousness, with its powers of rational reflection, is reached. It is no longer "right" for such a being to yield to the impulse of the moment, whether it regard self or others. The balance and harmony of individual life in its social setting ought now to be preserved, and the reason must pass judgment on each particular impulse. Here, then, the self-consciousness has a double function. The self is both judge and judged. In full comprehension of all its instincts, individual and social, it is called to pass a just and rational judgment on whatever instinct is seeking its satisfaction at the moment. But the instinctive life has far deeper roots than the rational, and has had a long start in the biological race. So arises the situation classically described in the apostle's words—"the good which I would I do not, but the evil which I would not, that I practise".[3] The result of such a divided heart can be the cry of spiritual suffering, "O, wretched man that I am! who shall deliver me out of the body of this death?" [4]

Our immediate interest, however, is not in the religious but in the social implications of the divided heart. The individual is "naturally" more inclined to

[3] Rom. VII. 19.
[4] Rom. VII. 24.

satisfy the impulses directly concerning himself than those which directly concern others and react only indirectly on his own satisfaction. He creates a little world of his own in which his self-consciousness is central. The degree of his concern for the welfare of others largely decides the quality of this self-consciousness, and this greater or less degree we recognize when we classify men roughly as "givers" or "getters"—those who impress us as generously eager to give, and those about whom we feel that at heart they are "selfish", whatever be the cloak of conventional decency or ostentatious liberality which hides this selfishness, perhaps even from themselves. Such classifications, however, are of the roughest kind and need to be made with constant readiness to abandon them. The inner consciousness of man (which is the most complete example of a unity we yet know) is so complex in its elements that our analysis is always imperfect. At best, we get a general impression of attitude, more or less distinct from the particular circumstances, just as in reading a book we get an impression of the author's outlook on life, simply from the way in which he faces his facts. It is in that inner attitude that the real quality of life consists. The actual significance of the life as satisfying or disappointing, as joyful or sorrowful, will depend far more on that inner attitude than on the data afforded by its social conditions—at any rate, after a minimum of necessary provision for these is reached.

One of the commonest reactions of this self-consciousness against the social order to which it belongs is in the assertion of its "rights". The individual of to-day, at any rate in the Western world, generally assumes that he is entitled to the social conditions which for him make life possible and worth while. These may range from "the living wage" to the fullest opportunity for education, from protection of life and limb against assault to the most ample provision for health and well-being, from security in tenure of property to adequate reward for individual attainments, from freedom for the expression of opinion to the accomplishment of the will of the majority in efficient government and administration. These claims are made in the name of "justice, not charity"; they are held to belong to the inalienable rights of the individual. Behind these quasi-instinctive claims of to-day, there lies a long history, showing how this individual consciousness of "rights" gradually emerged from an initial consciousness in which the emphasis fell relatively on the group to which the individual belonged. The word "relatively" is important, for we cannot conceive that in higher animals or in lower man there was ever a phase in which there was no individual consciousness. But all our historical evidence serves to show that the discovery of the individual (in our modern sense) was a slow process.[5] Early law, for example, often penalizes the whole group to which the offending individual belonged, as in the destruction of Achan's family because Achan had broken a taboo.[6] Even when, as in Greece, a strong sense of individuality was reached by a minority, the existence of a large slave population showed the limitation of the process. Feudalism, however explicable and valuable as a form of protection when it arose, implied a limitation of individuality by vassaldom. The power of a father over his child, once absolute, has been limited by legislation again and again down to our own times, in the interests of the individuality of the child. It is society itself which has slowly created what are called to-day the rights of the individual, society of course stimulated and guided by its most enlightened members. We cannot, therefore, justly argue about individual rights without remembering that they are social creations. Just as we cannot grow into individuals without social relations, so we cannot enjoy the amenities of that growth with-

[5] It may be illustrated by reference to the book called *The Individual in East and West*, edited by E. R. Hughes (1938) in which this process is traced in regard to primitive society, Greece, China, India, Israel and the Western world.

[6] Joshua VII. 25.

out some social order to protect them, whether they be material or spiritual. History has been defined by the Regius Professor of Modern History at Oxford as "the record of safety",[7] i.e., "the search for safety, for the conditions in which men may be free without being a danger to others".

Their rights are therefore always conditioned by their responsibilities for the social order on which those rights depend. It can be truly said that "the idea of the individual as a personality with rights as *against* society is . . . the creation of the recognition of him as endowed with rights *in* society".[8] Whatever meaning we may attach to "natural rights", they will depend for their validity on the kind of social order which the individual helps to constitute.

The cost of working out these rights even to the present imperfect stage of their expression has been the material and spiritual suffering which history records and imagination multiplies. With the significance of this cost for a religious view of the world we shall deal in later chapters. Here we note that progress to the freer expression of individuality and the effective assertion of its rights could come only by the painful clash of the individual with his group, or of one group with another. Spiritually, the keenest suf-

---

[7] *The Individual in East and West*, p. 174.

[8] J. H. Muirhead, in the *Encyclopaedia of Religion and Ethics*, Vol. X, p. 771.

fering has often come from the conflict of duties, which inevitably arises through the participation of the individual in more than one group, e.g., in both the family and the State. But that very conflict has put a keener edge on spiritual perception, from which the whole social order and ultimately all its individual members have benefited. We can hardly know the truth and worth of an idea until in one way or another we have fought for it, as Browning makes his hero [9] cry when entangled in a net of uncertainties, "The battle! That solves every doubt". The words are as true for a man's own divided heart as for the judgment of others.

The inseparability of rights and obligations may be put in another way when we think of the social inheritance of both good and evil into which we all enter. It is clearly irrational to complain of the evil unless we have balanced it against the good. This is no easy, perhaps no possible, calculation. Least of all are we likely to make it accurately whilst smarting under some present sense of injustice, some distribution of good or evil in the social order which affects us adversely. We are apt to dwell much more on the physical disability which may have handicapped us than on the faculties of body and mind which have had full activity in our life. We may think bitterly

[9] *Luria*, Act II, end.

of the chances that robbed us of a good education at the right time, and forget the later opportunities which we have been the more stimulated to use by the sense of an earlier loss. We may envy others the help of influential friends whilst forgetting how much we owe ourselves to the help we have actually received from others. Most of all are we likely to leave out of account the general good of social life that makes the permanent background to each of our more or less temporary troubles—the zest of human fellowship, the undeserved love and friendship of others, the accumulated knowledge and wisdom of past generations stored for us in institutions and especially in books—those "kings' treasuries" of which Ruskin wrote long since. It is not out of place here to quote his eloquent words about this great society of the past—words which have inspired not a few to the genuine study of great literature, as one of the greatest joys of life:—

"Into that you may enter always; in that you may take fellowship and rank according to your wish; from that, once entered into it, you can never be an outcast but by your own fault; by your aristocracy of companionship there, your own inherent aristocracy will be assuredly tested, and the motives with which you strive to take high place in the society of the living, measured, as to all the truth and sincerity

58

that are in them, by the place you desire in this company of the Dead." [10]

Whenever we consider these vast assets of actual or potential good which are ours as a social inheritance, reflection ought not only to check some of our hasty complaints about our own lot, but to lead us to a further thought—that each individual is a social unit, constituted the administrator and trustee of all the inheritance that is his, or can become his, "the thoughts of the wise, the labours of the good, the prayers of the devout". "Freely ye have received, freely give." Our debt for the manifold good which we have received from our forerunners can be repaid only to our contemporaries or descendants, and a right-minded man will not be happy unless he is doing something to repay this debt in the only possible way. The baseness of ingratitude is felt and acknowledged by all. In some ways, ingratitude is the worst of all sins, for it is selfishness sinning against the light of unselfishness. Perhaps nothing hurts us so much as to give of our best to another and to have it either flung back in contempt or appropriated in utter selfishness. How ashamed we ourselves feel when we discover that we have been wanting ourselves in gratitude to benefactors, even though this was through

[10] *Sesame and Lilies,* p. 20 of original edition.

ignorance! Much of the disinterested good wrought in the world, on the smallest or the largest scale, is surely prompted by this consciousness of what we owe to others, and it forms a motive which has been increasingly manifested in recent generations. But it is worth while to insist on these familiar truths—or truisms—because in every generation a large number of us are content to slink through life without any adequate recognition of what our social solidarity ought to mean (unless it concerns what others are expected to do for us).

Partly because of this unresponsive mass of mankind, all service means suffering. "Asked what was the first requisite for a Polytechnic, Mr Hogg replied, 'Somebody's heart's blood'; and his own was given." [11] It is in the ready, even joyous, acceptance of such sacrificial suffering that we see the chief dignity of man as a partner in the social order. A certain quality of selflessness marks all high achievement, a selflessness that may reach the seeming paradox of utter self-forgetfulness. It has found classical expression in two great passages of the Bible. One is that in which Moses [12] is represented as identifying himself with Israel after they have made the golden calf, and pleading with God, "Yet now if thou wilt forgive their

[11] C. Booth, *Life and Labour in London,* 3rd series, Vol. 7, p. 386.
[12] Ex. XXXII. 32.

sin—; and if not, blot me, I pray thee, out of thy book which thou hast written". The other is in the New Testament parallel, in which St Paul [13] writes:— "I could wish that I myself were anathema from Christ for my brethren's sake, my kinsmen according to the flesh". The paradox is, of course, that such a wish is impossible, in the nature of things—not simply because none of us can ever give himself a ransom for his brother in the realm of personal "salvation", but also because the very readiness to do so is the soul's best witness to its own entrance into larger life. If the line of thought of this chapter is justified, there can be no such thing as self-sacrifice in the strictest sense. That which bears the name is itself the fullest vindication of a self that has entered into social solidarity with its fellows and become most fully its true self.

It will be noticed that, in spite of the illustrations from religious life just given, self-sacrifice has here been urged simply as a part of social morality, the highest obligation it may entail. Whether such self-sacrifice can be fully and adequately evoked in the mass of mankind without the influence and sanctions of religion is another matter. So also is the question whether such a vision of social morality would have arisen at all but for some kind of religion. All that is

[13] Romans IX. 3.

here implied is that, simply on the basis of the relation of the individual to the society which incorporates him, it is rational and justifiable for him on occasion to sacrifice himself for the good of the community as the fullest realization of his own selfhood. Men have done it and will go on doing it in all the generations, and for the most varied apparent motives. But perhaps the underlying *rationale* of all the varieties is just the dim or clear recognition that the individual belongs to the race, not the race to the individual. Even for the achievement of the fullest individual life it is necessary to remember that

> "The game is more than the player of the game,
> And the ship is more than the crew."

The Parable of the Good Samaritan teaches us that men of the greatest respectability need to be reminded of larger horizons, and must continually be asking themselves the question, "Who is my neighbour?" In fact, for such men, the deepest rebuke to self-complacency is likely to come through the discovery of things left undone, rather than the remembrance of things done that ought not to have been done.[14] This rebuke comes to us with every enlargement of our

[14] Cf. *The Life of Mastery*, by G. Gordon, p. 144. He rightly emphasizes the value of reading biographies.

social circle, every discovery of what we might have been and ought to have been to others. For most men, the life of the family is the chief and primary place in which to learn this truth about ourselves. But it is not only in the family that the lesson is learnt. Bacon's famous aphorism, "He that hath Wife and Children hath given Hostages to Fortune", applies to a wider circle also. Every friendship we make is not only a possible enrichment, but also a possible source of suffering to us. We cannot have the spiritual wealth of wide and deep social relations unless we are ready to pay their spiritual cost in the sacrifices of love. To realize that is one way of approaching the agony of Gethsemane; the love of Jesus for His fellows was the deepest measure of His suffering.

Thus we see that the principle of vicarious suffering is deep-based in our very nature as men. It is inevitable, so far as we share at all really in the common life of men. The spread of an epidemic or the distribution of gas masks is, in the physical realm, a sermon on the text that none of us liveth to himself. On the higher level of spiritual consciousness, we can indeed choose the life of selfish isolation, and escape from the suffering entailed by social sympathies—at the heavy cost of missing the best of life. But if we choose the good part, then the privileges and the perils must go hand in hand. But spiritual growth is characterized by a subtle power of re-adjustment to the increasing demands of a larger life, that larger life into which it has entered by its very growth. In a richer sense than that of the ancient tribal promise, it discovers that "as thy days so shall thy strength be".[15]

[15] Deut. XXXIII. 25.

CHAPTER V

SUFFERING AND SIN

WE ARE sometimes told that Jesus said little about sin, and that His disciples have made too much of it. To this we may reply that Jesus did not need to say much, for sin said it all in crucifying Him. Sin is seen most clearly in its issues.

One reason why the Cross of Christ has so wrought on the consciences of men is that it exhibits the true character of moral evil by expressing it in terms of suffering, which all can understand. The sins of men actually crucified Jesus—the sins of the Jewish Sanhedrin, which were jealousy and prejudice, the sin of Judas who betrayed Him, the sin of Peter who denied Him, the sin of Pontius Pilate, who found injustice easier than justice, the sin of Roman soldiers, who added mocking to His scourging and crucifixion. These are *our* sins as much as theirs—jealousy, prejudice, disloyalty, time-serving, pitilessness—though the consequences are not so clearly seen, when *we* are the sinners. Yet, in similar circumstances, without the light that history has flung upon the Cross, any of us might do like deeds. But just because the result of those ancient sins is revealed in the suffering of the Cross, we are made to see what sin really is. Sin is something that can do things like *that*.

"Sin" is properly a religious term denoting moral evil in its relation to God, a transgression of His law. We describe moral evil as "crime" when it conflicts with the human law of a land. But what is moral evil in itself? Perhaps the most frequent definition is that it is the abuse of human freedom in the interests of the self.[1] This pre-supposes that we *are* in some measure free. But if we are not, then it is idle to speak of moral evil at all, in distinction from physical and psychical evil. Morality implies responsibility and responsibility implies freedom. A large part of the world's suffering is due to the abuse of freedom by the human will possessing it. No judgment about suffering is worth anything which does not make a clear distinction between that which springs from the evil will of man and that which seems to belong to Nature as such, for which God is more directly responsible. In this chapter we are concerned only with suffering in its various relations with moral evil.

One initial prejudice, to which earlier reference has

[1] Against the theory of moral evil as negation—the absence of good, we should note that neither good nor evil are more than abstractions until expressed in good or evil agents (cf. Tennant, *Philosophical Theology*, II, 182).

been made, should be put aside. It is that we are argu-
ing in a circle when we say that moral evil is a cause
of suffering, after virtually defining it as socially and
individually harmful. That is partly true and it is inevitable. The discovery of moral evil has to be made
slowly through its results for the individual or for the
society. But once discovered, deeper connections reveal themselves. The social judgment that certain
kinds of action are harmful to the society, a judgment
confirmed by some sort of penalty, is not the end of
the matter. Some of these primitive tabus are meaningless to a later generation and sooner or later are
dropped. But others prove to have some inner and intrinsic justification, which enables them to endure and
to find relatively permanent acceptance by the individual, though, perhaps, with a change of explanation.

Suffering and sin keep close company. Suffering is
linked to evil in the spiritual sphere much as in the
physical, where disease brings suffering. Moral evil
may be represented as a disease of personality which
inevitably and intrinsically hampers or destroys life
whether in the individual or in the society. Is this generally true? It is certainly true of sensuality, in any of
its forms—gluttony, drunkenness, sexual lust. Here
the excessive indulgence in sensuous pleasure is bound
to entail suffering, sooner or later, for it is an abuse of
the physical organism, which Nature vindicates. But

it is no less true, if less apparent, when we examine spiritual faults such as selfishness. Not only is this an offence against social solidarity which brings its inevitable harvest of unpopularity and even active opposition, but, in subtle ways, it registers spiritual deterioration in the body also, as we may see from the faces of many selfish people.[2]

It is a strange comment on the facility with which we men extract moral evil from Nature's gifts to us that the four men who were in smaller or greater degree concerned in the earlier developments of anaesthesia, viz., C. W. Long, H. Wells, C. T. Jackson and W. Morton, in the 'forties of the last century, all came to an unhappy end, largely, as it seems, through the jealousy and strife and hatred which this most beneficent discovery engendered. Wells committed suicide in prison. Long died suddenly in embitterment. Jackson's hatred of Morton is said to have brought him to the lunatic asylum. Morton died from a stroke induced by reading one of Jackson's attacks on him.[3] Over against this melancholy record, however, we

[2] The body is a more integral part of personality than is usually recognized, and the interaction of mind and body in suffering is much more than we realize. Doctors tell us of "the fine threads connecting mental agitation, depression and anxieties with the numerous disturbances of the organs of circulation, digestion and sex" (*The Doctor and His Patients*, by Albert Krecke, E. T. by M. M. Green, p. 27).

[3] The facts are set out at length in the interesting book called *Triumph over Pain*, by René Fülöp-Miller, trans. by Eden and Cedar Paul (1938): see, especially, p. 322.

68

ought to set such conduct as that of Professor and Madame Curie, who, as everybody knows, refused to make private profit from their discovery of radium, in spite of their straitened circumstances.[4]

In view of the deterioration so often visibly produced by moral evil, we may describe it (in one of its aspects) as "vice", i.e., something inherently and intrinsically corruptive. This implies that moral evil is self-destructive,[5] however long the process of corruption may take. It does not necessarily imply that the evil will ceases altogether to exist, but that it loses its higher attributes and finer capacities, including its freedom.

The mental and spiritual deterioration caused by moral evil is well illustrated by the familiar lines of Burns:—[6]

> "I wave the quantum o' the sin;
> The hazard of concealing;
> But Och! it hardens a' within
> And petrifies the feeling!"

The "hardening" and the accompanying atrophy of conscience undoubtedly lessens the spiritual discom-

[4] *Madame Curie*, by Eve Curie, trans. by Vincent Sheean (1938), pp. 214, 223.

[5] Cf. J. Martineau, *A Study of Religion*, II, p. 109, and F. R. Tennant, *Philosophical Theology*, Vol. II, p. 194. The latter points out that the intrinsic nature of good and evil protects God's purpose from defeat. The good is self-conservative; the evil is essentially unstable.

[6] *Epistle to a Young Friend*.

fort of the evil-doer, in some instances almost to van-
ishing-point. The measure of it can be known by the
pains of a re-awakened spiritual circulation, which
are not less acute in their own sphere than those of
long-cramped limbs.

Anyone who has been brought into a deep consciousness of his own sinfulness will know that the
spiritual suffering which this involves is more than
any physical pain, more than any of the disappointments and tragedies of life. It is *the* tragedy of life,
though many do not, especially to-day, face it and
call it such. They feel a certain discomfort that they
are not better than they are; they are sorry for some
of the things they have done. But, lacking the clearer
teaching of former days, which they dismiss as ex-
ploded dogma, they turn away from this discomfort
and dismiss it as a mere survival, or an inevitable accompaniment of life. Anything more definite, such as
theology calls "guilt", they regard as a subjective illusion, an artificial result of antiquated teaching. The
evolutionary view of sin seems to confirm this, together with the thought that "I am not worse than
many other people". But if we resolutely face God
in the testimony of conscience, if our ideal is high
enough to be a continual rebuke to our achievement,
if we give the Christian Gospel a chance of proving
itself true, we shall not be content with such excuses

or evasions. We shall be compelled, sooner or later, to cry with Paul "O wretched man that I am! who shall deliver me from this body of death?"

How ought we to think of the relation of suffering to sin? Let us begin by thinking of the proper relation of suffering to crime in human law. What is the right theory of the punishment of criminals? Most people would agree to-day that it should be both deterrent and reformatory; that it should check crime by the fear of its penalty, and that it should also aim at creating a good citizen out of the offender, whether by direct effect or by the opportunities supplied by the conditions under which the penalty is administered. But is it also retributory? Is the suffering inflicted to be conceived as something also demanded by "justice" in the full sense, something which the criminal has "deserved"?

The answers to this question are sharply opposed and strongly maintained. Rashdall, for example,[7] holds that the retributive theory is "a mere survival of by-gone modes of thought". It is, he says, impossible to decide what exact desert is. The only value of the principle is to express the resentment of the community against wrong-doing and the spiritual purpose of the State. Punishment is justifiable only as deterrent and reformatory (educative). The fear of it does help

[7] *The Theory of Good and Evil*, Bk. I, Ch. IX.

71

to make men better by strengthening the higher self against the lower. But the retributive theory "shows a disrespect for human personality by proposing to sacrifice human life and human Well-being to a lifeless fetich styled the Moral Law". Is this strong condemnation justified? Surely we may answer that the historical origin of a principle does not decide its ultimate truth [8] and that, if the principle is maintained, the exact amount of punishment is of secondary importance and can reasonably be controlled by other considerations (including the protection of society and the reform of the criminal). It is, in fact, a false antithesis to contrast the principle of retribution with those of deterrence and reformation, as though they were exclusive. As for the attitude taken towards the dignity of human personality, we may fairly claim that we respect it more by the recognition of moral desert than by decrying any application of the moral law to it.

The right standpoint is that maintained by Dr Edwyn Bevan, in his recent Gifford Lectures.[9] He argues that the true deterrent is the just anger of the community, expressed and reinforced in the penalty for the crime. In this penalty desert is always implicit. It

[8] Cf. Westermarck, *The Origin and Development of the Moral Ideas*, Chs. II and III. He defends the principle of retribution.

[9] *Symbolism and Belief*, pp. 218 ff.

72

is no valid objection to say that there is much bad desert which escapes punishment, or that none of us is good enough to condemn another. The moral order is more than the individual, and his reformation depends on his recognition of justice. This is an apprehension of Reality by the human spirit. As for the further point urged by Rashdall, that the principle of retribution leaves no room for the Christian doctrine of forgiveness, Dr Bevan's answer is that "there would be nothing for God to forgive if there were no bad desert". We may also add here that the Christian doctrine of God does not proclaim an abstract Law of Righteousness as something external to Him. We can say with Dale:—[10] "In God the law is *alive;* it reigns on His throne, sways His sceptre, is crowned with His glory".

Our attitude towards the retributive principle as it affects human justice is likely to influence our interpretation of the divine justice. Those who dismiss this principle in the one sphere are not likely to find it in the other. This is not the proper place to discuss the retributive justice of God, which will concern us in later chapters.[11] All that needs to be claimed here is that, as Denney argues,[12] there is a reaction of the

[10] *The Atonement,* p. 372.
[11] IX, X.
[12] *The Christian Doctrine of Reconciliation,* p. 207.

universe against sin which is "instinctively appreciated by conscience". Each of us can be, and often is, conscious that he has deserved, as a just penalty, such suffering as has come to him. The recognition of this stills all complaint, whilst repentance of the wrongdoing changes the penalty into discipline. Only here and there perhaps can we prove a connection of cause and effect in another man's life. But, from within our own, we are on surer ground. Here the ultimate religious fact is always the unity that emerges from our reaction to circumstance, not the mere circumstance alone. Biologically, a broken leg is an evil, but morally or religiously we cannot characterize it until we know what is the individual response to this apparent "misfortune". The enforced inaction might serve to embitter the whole subsequent life, or it might give just the needed opportunity for "recollection", and become the moral or religious watershed. The man might then regard his "misfortune" as both "penalty" for wholly selfish ambitions which it may have frustrated, and "discipline" into a better life. From the higher level of faith in divine control of circumstances, he would be fully justified—because *he knows the fact from within*. In such unity of experience, the providence of God will often find a sufficient vindication, unknown to the mere spectator.

In our own times, it is the spectacle of the suffering caused by certain features of our civilization which most forcibly brings home to men in general the nature of moral evil. Indeed it may be that the moral reaction from the phenomena of war, unemployment and bad housing conditions is the way by which the lost sense of sin will be recovered. Any thoughtful man can see, for example, that war is often the product of a false pride in nationalism or of selfish individual ambition, and that the vested interests of armament manufacture can easily become a contributory cause. But such motives are not peculiar to international relations; they are simply the working out of individual morals on a large scale.

Let us freely admit that the largeness of the scale introduces new factors and more intractable elements. It is little use to demand from pulpit or platform that international morality ought to be brought up to the Christian level unless we also recognize the necessary differences between the action of a society and that of an individual. Nor must we dispose of such matters by saying that if the majority of individuals composing a national society were properly converted, the action of the society would be right.[13] Even if it were, the international problem would remain. The menace

[13] The necessarily clumsy methods of democracy hardly guarantee this result, which might indeed follow more quickly by the action of a benevolent dictator.

of war is now presented to us as a world-problem, which no single nation can hope to solve, still less any individual.

All this, however, must not rob us of our sense of individual responsibility in the last resort. It *is* the moral evil of individuals which is the ultimate cause of the sufferings involved in war or bad social conditions. They may seem more or less inevitable under an existent system, but that, if proved, would mean only that the system itself ought to be changed. Here the skill of the expert is necessary to carry out the good will of the individual. But it is the bad will of the individual,—not God, save as the ultimate source of man's moral freedom—that is responsible for a vast amount of the world's suffering. That bad will we may as well call by its old-fashioned name of "sin".

The suffering of mankind reaches its visible limit in death. Has this event in the history of the individual any relation to moral evil? The biological answer would certainly deny this, except in the case of such abuse of the physical organism as involved premature death. For biology, death is a purely physical event belonging to the history of the organism, the result of its failure to respond effectively to its environment through the gradual degeneration of its cell-structure. The death of the individual is a necessary feature of the progress of the race, so that death can be called "the servant of life".[14] On the other hand, primitive man has usually regarded death as an unnatural intrusion. The mythology of many peoples tries to explain why there should be death at all.[15] This is not the view taken in the Old Testament, notwithstanding the threat of Genesis II. 17, that disobedience to the divine prohibition will entail death. In point of fact, the suggestion of the story is that man is naturally mortal; his expulsion from Eden is to prevent him from gaining immortality by eating the fruit of the tree of life (III. 22ff.). It is not until the second century B.C. that we see the rise in Jewish theology of the belief that human death is due to the initial act of disobedience:—

> "From a woman was the beginning of sin;
> And because of her we all die." [16]

A similar view is taken by St Paul in Rom. V. 12, where it is stated that death (not sin) has become the universal lot of mankind, because of the sin of its representative (in whom the race was summed up, according to the current ideas of "corporate personality"). Attempts to reconcile this belief with the biological view of death are as mistaken as attempts

[14] J. Y. Simpson, *The Spiritual Interpretation of Nature*, p. 94.
[15] Many examples will be found in *The Encyclopaedia of Religion and Ethics*, IV, 411 ff.
[16] Ecclus. XXV, 24.

77

to reconcile Genesis with geology. But we are warranted in saying that death challenges man's attachment to this world, "the lust of the flesh, and the lust of the eyes, and the vainglory of life",[17] and also completes the Christian's deliverance from "this body of death".[18] In this sense it may have profound spiritual significance,[19] as marking the end of one chapter of life and the beginning of another, though in itself merely a physical and natural event. So far as death is regarded as an immediate prelude to divine judgment, it may also profoundly affect the conscience of man. But this is not the same thing as implying that death itself is the penalty of guilt. It must be recognized, of course, that any event in the history of the physical organism will have a meaning for the spiritual being to whom it belongs different from its significance for the animal. But the religious conception of death is a new estimate dependent on the personal attitude to it, and not something wholly "objective", as the penalty theory would imply.

These remarks apply also to the belief underlying Rom. VIII. 18-25—the very impressive conception of "the whole creation groaning and travailing together" and involved in "the bondage of corruption" as a result

[17] I John II. 16.
[18] Rom. VII. 24.
[19] *Die Religion im Geschichte und Gegenwart*, V. 1202.

of man's sin. If we mean by these phrases that Nature does present its own problem of suffering, that is true enough. Or again, the conception may suggest to us the true thought that Nature is incomplete without man and man's redemption, in which a justification will be found for all the travail. But this is something quite different from the view that sin is the *cause* of Nature's suffering. To explain it by that we should have to adopt some such theory as that put forward by Professor N. P. Williams, that there has been "a pre-cosmic vitiation of the whole Life-Force", a "Fall" of the "World-Soul" from which has issued both Nature and man.[20]

It keeps us nearer the facts we know to say that the exercise and abuse of human freedom is something which, from the very nature of freedom, we cannot explain, save by its own causality. To explain man's sinfulness by a "Fall" either within or prior to the history of the world would really destroy moral responsibility, just as much as an evolutionary theory of sin, which would make it a necessary stage in man's development. The same consideration rules out all dogma as to the final outcome, the ultimate destiny of man-

---

[20] *The Ideas of the Fall and of Original Sin*, pp. 523, 526, 529. We may refer here to the Hindu doctrine of *Karma* and the transmigration of the soul (noting the differences from the above view). The pre-suppositions of the *Karma* doctrine are too alien to the Christian faith to make any contribution to our subject.

kind. We can be sure that sin brings suffering, but whether that suffering will ultimately lead to the change of all evil wills into good, no one has the right to say.

It is better not to speculate about "Everlasting Punishment" or "Universal Restoration" or "Conditional Immortality". Perhaps the last comes nearest to the implicates of the New Testament doctrine that "Eternal Life" is the gift of God through Christ, a quality of life rather than a quantity. We may, if we like, find some confirmation for this in the fact already noted, that moral evil does destroy the higher capacities of the spirit of man, just as moral good develops them, and suggests the possibility of a much richer development beyond death. On the other hand, spiritual deterioration cannot be identified with complete self-extinction. "Evil cannot destroy the soul in the way disease destroys the body; its effect is more like to a perpetual distortion." [21] It may be that the last penalty of sin is the complete loss of moral freedom, and with it of personality, as Martineau suggests.[22] It is remarkable that the gentle spirit of Whittier should have contemplated such a possibility, in that heart-searching poem of his called "The Answer":—

[21] M. C. D'Arcy, *The Pain of This World and the Providence of God*, p. 43.
[22] *A Study of Religion*, II, p. 108.

"Forever round the Mercy-seat
　　The guiding lights of Love shall burn;
But what if, habit-bound, thy feet
　　Shall lack the will to turn?

"What if thine eye refuse to see,
　　Thine ear of Heaven's free welcome fail,
And thou a willing captive be,
　　Thyself thy own dark jail?"

Finally, our present survey ought to include some reference to the extra-human world, and its relation to this, as affecting our problem. How far is the suffering of mankind due to malignant spirits? To some readers, it may seem an utter anachronism to put the question at all; does not the belief in demons belong to the limbo of banished superstitions? Yet we should remember that Jesus took the demonic world and its ruler, the devil, seriously enough, and that He traced many of the sufferings of mankind to demonic influence, which it was a central part of His work, and His disciples' work, to overthrow.[23] The story of His temptation frames the picture of His life in a conflict with invisible, as well as with visible, powers. Similar beliefs run through the whole of the New Testament and have continued in the Christian Church more or less into our own times. Those who do not

[23] Matt. XII. 28, etc.

realize the intensity with which they were held in the
early centuries should read the chapter on "The Conflict with the Demons" in Harnack's *Mission and Ex-
pansion of Christianity*.[24] Now, so far as the *form* of
such beliefs goes, we may readily explain it in the
consciousness of Jesus as part of the conditions under
which "the Word became flesh and dwelt amongst
us". An acceptance, genuine and sincere, of much of
the thought-world of His generation was as necessary
as His acceptance of an Aramaic speech and a Jewish
peasant's dress. But the emphasis of the Gospels on
this belief compels us to consider whether, apart from
the particular form, the substance of belief in "the
devil and all his angels" does not contain some sub-
stantial truth. The Christian believes in good influences which emanate from the larger cosmic order
encompassing his earthly life; it is not therefore in itself unreasonable to admit the possibility of evil influences from the same sphere. The fact that one spiritual being can be influenced by another for evil as well
as for good is only too familiar within the human
society; to believe in such influence on a larger scale
simply extends the field, provided man's ultimate
freedom of choice is safeguarded. We have, of course,
means of waging war with both physical and mental
disease much more efficient than those of the ancient

[24] *Die Mission und Ausbreitung des Christentums*, Bk. II, Ch. III.

exorcist. But the phenomena of moral retrogression, in both nations and individuals, may well make us chary of "denying the devil his due". All that it is necessary to urge is that, for the Christian faith, there can be no dualism. The range of moral and spiritual conflict may extend, for anything we know, far beyond our earth, and even beyond our universe. Rebellion against God may be just as possible elsewhere as it is here. But faith in the God and Father of Jesus Christ demands that the ultimate victory be securely His, and that He have no permanent rival on earth or in heaven.

CHAPTER VI

PROVIDENCE AND NATURE

IN THIS and the two following chapters, our concern
will be with three different realms of God's relation
to human suffering, and we shall escape much confu-
sion and even anxiety if we clearly distinguish them.
Flurried and anxious people are generally those who
are trying to do several things at once, or at least to
think of doing them. They are like the multiple musi-
cian we may have seen in the street, who plays on
pipes with his mouth, an accordion with his hands,
the drum on his back by sticks fastened to his elbows,
cymbals on his head by a cord fastened to his heels.
But he never finds his way as an efficient soloist to
the concert platform. The shops sometimes offer us a
multiple tool, pincers, wrench, hammer, file, screw-
driver and nail-extractor all in one. But when we
have pinched our fingers whilst trying to drive a
screw, we are likely to demand a simpler tool which
will do one thing well. Concentration on the single
issue is always one of the secrets of effective thought
or action. When Isaac Newton was asked about his

own marvellous insight, he said that "if he differed from other men the difference perhaps lay in his capacity to pay attention to a problem".[1] In a recently discovered letter, a friend of David Livingstone wrote of him, "He was pre-eminently a Man—patient and enduring under hardships—content to win his way by inches, but never swerving from it—gentle, kindly, brotherly to the children of the land—absolutely calm and unruffled amidst danger and difficulty, and satisfied to see but one step in advance—if ever man carried out the scriptural injunction to take no thought for the morrow—that man was David Livingstone".[2]

The application of this to our present subject may be put into the words of a familiar Latin tag—"*divide et impera*". The right answer always depends on putting the right question, and this in turn on its own division into separate questions. The problem of suffering can be as slippery as an eel if we do not decide just what part of it we mean to grasp and hold firmly. We have already seen that a not inconsiderable part of the world's suffering is due to man's abuse of his own freedom. We have also seen that man's vulnerability to suffering through the actions or fortunes of others is inseparable from the social life of mankind, with all its undoubted gains and blessings. Here we

[1] *Isaac Newton*, by J. W. N. Sullivan, p. 12.
[2] *Times Literary Supplement*, Sept. 4, 1936.

85

are concerned with the world-order as it might present itself to a detached spectator. Of course, no such spectator really exists; he is at most a useful abstraction to enable us to focus attention on one aspect of the problem, without being flurried and overwhelmed by half-a-dozen others. There is the more need of concentration here because this is the point at which wrong judgments are most likely. We are apt to look at this or that individual "hard case", and begin to generalize from it, and still more apt, perhaps, to argue from our own personal misfortunes. The latter point of view will be considered in a subsequent chapter. Here we need only remind ourselves that the problem is at this stage a purely intellectual one. It should be quite unaffected by the fact that the suffering in question is *my* suffering. For the purpose of this chapter *I* am a negligible atom, a mere unit amongst astronomic figures, and not the creative centre of a little world of my own. The question before us is this—how far can Nature, with all the physical suffering which it entails, be reconciled with the moral demands of a higher level?

One truth, at least, we may carry over from the experiences of the individual man or woman to that of the vast uncounted multitude of mankind, viz., the intimate, indeed the inseparable, association of mind and body. Whatever happens to these mortal millions after death, their personality in present experience is inseparable from a body. They are therefore subject to all the "laws", that is to the observed regularities, of the physical order. It is not necessarily cynical to say that "The dearest moments of life, reduced to scientific terms, become nothing but the most mocking action of a few nerve-centres".[3] Whatever else those moments are, they have their physiological basis. It is not an army only that marches on its stomach; the saintliest mystic, "breathless with adoration", is also anchored in the body. The great apostle, filled with an imperial ambition for his master's cause, and caught up into the third heaven, must sink back to the painful reality of "a stake in the flesh".

1. Through our bodies, then, we make inevitable and necessary contact with the physical order, in which regularity is the most obvious feature. The term may be taken to cover "the precision, impartiality and inevitability of the Laws of Nature".[4] Without such regularity, life as we know it would be impossible. This is true even on the level of mere existence. Every breath we take depends on the regularity of physical law. The life-giving air supplying its oxygen to the lungs, the circulation of the cleansed blood, the chemical processes by which food is digested and

[3] Putnam Weale, *The Revolt*, p. 167.
[4] E. W. Johnson, *Suffering, Punishment and Atonement*, p. 188.

the blood-supply maintained, the transformation of potential into actual physical energy—all these, which make our life possible, are ours because of the regularity of Nature. But we owe far more to this regularity than mere existence. To the discipline of Nature we owe our power to think rationally, to calculate and foresee, to draw analogies and reason from cause to effect.[5] Physical nature cannot explain the mystery of consciousness, but always conditions it, builds its cradle, and becomes the teacher through whose guidance mind can develop. We have only to try to conceive a world of pure chance, utterly irregular, and with no sequence of cause and effect in order to realize this.[6] The only physical world we know is a world of law and order, and we must learn to take that for granted in our theory, as we all take it for granted in actual life.

How far is there similar or parallel "Natural Law in the Spiritual World"?[7] How far, for example, does the saying, "whatsoever a man soweth, that shall he also reap", apply to moral as well as to agricultural activity? That there is considerable truth in it few would deny, however much men may complain of its

[5] See Tennant's valuable emphasis on this point in his *Philosophical Theology*, II., p. 200.

[6] Cf. the amusing example of such an attempt in Dr Todd's *Truth Made Simple* (1839) called "Hafed's Dream".

[7] The title of Henry Drummond's once famous book.

PROVIDENCE AND NATURE

operation when it affects themselves disastrously. We
have seen something of this in considering the relation of suffering and sin; [8] physical suffering usually
follows from the abuse of physical organs, and mental suffering has often its own more subtle links of
cause and effect, e.g., the suffering due to the unpopularity of selfishness, and its isolation from all the
joys of comradeship and social fellowship. But though
we may believe that there is ultimately a spiritual order, not less "regular" than the physical, we cannot
immediately argue from one to another, except by
way of illustrative analogy, as in the sowing of seed.
Moral and spiritual life is far more complex in its factors, and far less open to observation and experiment
than is the physical order. Moreover, the apparently
new factor of freedom introduces incalculable elements, elements which can be called non-rational. Our
moral and spiritual life is as yet at a low stage of development, as compared with the physical body,
which seems to have had so long a start in the cosmic
race. On this higher level, we are as yet but learners,
and Nature with her unbroken regularities is our
great teacher, and perhaps at last our great ideal.
What then of "miracle"—the kind of miracle we instinctively invoke when we suffer as the result of
Nature's regularity? Why should there not be some

[8] Ch. V.

89

divine intervention to break the chain of physical cause and effect? Would not that often seem to be the true justification of providence, when the sufferer is wholly innocent, and is simply caught up into this remorseless sequence without any moral blame?

Here let us remember what was said about dealing with one difficulty at a time. We are not now considering the inner world of the individual sufferer; to do that fairly we must take into account the whole of his individual life and attitude and especially his personal reaction to suffering. We are here considering the world-order as a whole, the mass of its suffering so far as due to the regularity of its process. If we steadily keep to that point of view for the moment, we shall see that a world of such "miracles" would become a contradiction in terms, for a world without regularity would not be an ordered world or "cosmos" at all. This is not meant to suggest any denial of the supernatural, or of miracle as the working of higher "law", on the higher level of the personal relation of God and man.[9] But it does imply that we cannot have

[9] In that relation, prayer is man's conscious or unconscious appeal to God, and "miracle" is God's answer to man's need, whatever the form of its mediation in the course of His providence. Some of the answers may seem to us "interventions", but that "living garment of God" woven on "the roaring loom of time" by which we see Him, will always be a seamless robe. The closer our personal relation to God, the more clearly we shall realize this, in the transformed unity of experience. For a fuller discussion of this personal relation see Professor H. H. Farmer's book, *The World and God*.

two incompatibles at once—a world of fixed order on which our very existence depends, and from which we have gained the very capacity to think at all, and a world full of miraculous interventions, in which "miracle" would become a commonplace. The fallacy lies in thinking of this or that individual, as though he constituted the whole of the world. Part of the truth at least lies in frankly recognising that the physical ills from which men suffer spring from the working of Nature's beneficent regularity as much as do those of her "gifts" in which we most rejoice.

This, one will say, is cold comfort for the sufferer himself, and so it is. But it is cold comfort just because religion, and in particular the Christian faith, has taught us to look for something better, and to find a warmer comfort. Let us remember that men of a nobler build than most of us have been strengthened to endure suffering by this very thought of Nature's unchanging ways. I am thinking in particular of the Stoics. The slave Epictetus can bid us "Seek not to have things happen as you choose them, but rather choose them to happen as they do, and so shall you live prosperously".[10] The Emperor Marcus Aurelius writes to the same effect of the true Stoic:—"Those things that are his own, and in his own power, he himself takes order, for that they be good: and as for

[10] *The Teaching of Epictetus,* translated by T. W. Rolleston, p. 81.

those that happen unto him, he believes them to be so".[11] There is a real strength to be won from the acceptance of Nature's inexorable regularity as the condition of our life, and it is not to be despised because, as the Christian believes, there is something beyond this, something into which its truth is taken up and transformed. But we cannot have the Christian comfort without the Christian faith—and here we are facing the difficulties created by suffering for those who believe in divine providence, but are without the Christian interpretation of it. All the human sufferings which Martineau classifies as environmental [12]—those due to earthquake and volcano, storm, flood, frost, avalanche, epidemic and endemic diseases—all these belong to Nature's regularity. Their appearance is often sudden and catastrophic, but they are the result of long preparation. The storm that destroys a harvest and brings famine is as much the regular product of meteorological law as the harvest it destroys is the product of agricultural law. It would be an enormous boon to mankind if the malaria mosquito could be exterminated, and civilization wage successful warfare against the micro-organism that causes malignant cholera. Yet these "enemies" of man are exceptional products of a biological order which is the condition

[11] *Meditations*, III, 4, p. 21 of Casaubon's translation in Everyman's Library.
[12] *A Study of Religion*, Vol. II, pp. 83ff.

of our life. It is inevitable that we should say of death by cholera "it is intolerable agony, and it is not right that human beings should suffer so much".[13] Yet before we indict Nature for her criminals, we should remember the far greater number of her well-behaved citizens and the general beneficence of her ordered ways. This also is the place to recall Nature's great ministry of spiritual healing, however we explain it. There are not a few, whether through temperament or through circumstances, who turn from the world of men to the world of Nature in their time of trouble and gain relief in these ordered ways and in the beauty through which they find their expression. Wordsworth is the apostle of this ministry, and his own faith is given as simply as anywhere in a sonnet to a brook:—

> "It seems the Eternal Soul is clothed in thee
> With purer robes than those of flesh and blood,
> And hath bestowed on thee a safer good;
> Unwearied joy, and life without its cares." [14]

2. A second aspect of Nature that concerns us is her dynamic quality. We live in a universe of active forces and constant motion. Modern physics has shown this to be as true for the realm of inanimate

[13] Victor Bayley, *Nine-Fifteen from Victoria*, p. 147.
[14] *Miscellaneous Sonnets*, Pt. II, XXXI.

matter, with its electrons and radiations, as biology had already shown in regard to the evolution of species. The relatively unchanging pattern of the starry sky above us and of the everlasting hills around us suggests a "tranquillity" that conceals the "toil" of Nature.[15] In truth, there is nothing static about Nature—unless it be in the fixity of the hidden goal to which Nature is moving.

This characteristic of movement is, of course, no guarantee of progress. But it does ensure the continuance of vitality and re-adjustment, and does forbid the settling down to an existence without adventure. In the biological realm, in particular, Nature is always saying, "Move on!—or fall out and die by the wayside".[16] That unswerving command causes a large amount of the world's suffering. Weakness and inefficiency—by Nature's own standards—are "ruthlessly" trampled on; the race that is no longer biologically efficient dies out. Hunger, thirst and pain in general are beneficent warnings and essential stimuli to action, as we have already seen,[17] and they belong to Nature's immanent purpose expressed in its policeman's command, "Move on". The "purpose" we may ascribe to Nature is in full harmony with the persistent purpose

[15] Cf. Matthew Arnold's sonnet "Quiet Work":—"Still do thy sleepless ministers move on".

[16] Cf. the stirring close of Emerson's essay on "Compensation".

[17] Ch. II.

94

in a human life, with all the price of toil and suffering it may have to pay. It is "deep calling unto deep"
—a modern equivalent to the ancient Stoic principle
of Nature calling man to live in harmony with her.
Such a purpose in man is not necessarily moral at all,
and may be as ruthless in fact as is Nature in appearance. But just as we should explain the hardships
borne by a man and the price he pays in suffering by
the strength of his dominating purpose, so we may
largely explain the suffering that Nature exhibits in the
animal and human world by what answers in Nature
to conscious purpose in man. There is constant movement, at any cost. Whether that movement will issue
in real progress depends on other considerations which
do not at the moment concern us. But movement of
some kind is essential to progress, and Nature is just
as emphatic on movement as on regularity.

With animal suffering for its own sake, this book,
as its title indicates, is not directly concerned. But
every thoughtful and sympathetic observer would allow that it is a serious element in the problem of a
providential order. It is probable that we greatly ex-
aggerate the sufferings of many of the animals, whose
physiological apparatus for suffering seems so much
more limited than ours, and that we fail to allow for
the great increase in the capacity for suffering due to
human self-consciousness, and its power to look before

and after (see Ch. I). But even so, we are left with a residuum of animal suffering that is unconsciously vicarious. It is part of the price of Nature's "progress" in evolving more elaborate types, including man himself. We need not complicate our problem by dwelling on the "rights" of dumb creatures, and ignoring the vast amount of pleasure that is theirs, in quantity, at least, more than overbalancing the pain. But we do well to remember the social factor here,[18] and this is so important that it deserves separate consideration in regard to divine providence.

3. We may speak of "corporate structure" as a third characteristic of Nature's ways, in continuation of her regularity and dynamism. It is true that Nature is an arena of unceasing strife and can be truly depicted as "red in tooth and claw". That holds of the vegetable as well as of the animal world. As Albert Schweitzer says, "There is always going on in the primaeval forest, though without a sound to betray it, an uncanny struggle between creepers and trees. Anything which cannot work its way up above the creeper-growth into the sunlight dies a slow and painful death".[19] But before we condemn Nature as utterly unsocial, let us remember that man himself, in whom sociality is as fundamental an element as indi-

[18] Cf. Ch. IV.
[19] *More from the Primaeval Forest*, p. 121.

viduality, is still imperfectly social, and usually confines his sociality to narrow groups, just as do animals. One of the greatest practical issues before the world at the present time, perhaps the greatest, is to learn how to inter-relate the values of nationalism with the necessity of internationalism. The secret of world-peace and the avoidance of war lies there. We can hardly throw stones, then, at Nature, because she has not progressed beyond ourselves.

Within the narrower group the law of the herd holds. There is the maternal and protective instinct to be reckoned with. The sociality of Nature, like our own, is very limited, but like our own, it is real so far as it goes. Within the narrow limits there is abundant evidence of corporate structure. Nature has seen to it that there is due provision for the continuance of the generations, even at the cost of travail-pangs. By the side of the instinct of self-protection, there is that of the nurture and defence of the young. When longer care is needed, as in the case of the human infant, a richer network of conscious relations is created, able to meet the new need. If Nature seems "careless of the single life" it is because she is so careful of the whole group, so anxious to secure its continuance and welfare.

We may say with confidence, concerning Nature's ways as a whole, what has been said of Pasteur's discoveries:—"These laws display much more than 'a survival of the fittest'; and if they discover in Nature a battlefield, they discover also loyalties and devotions by which aggregations of life in the higher organisms are transmuted into forms resembling in many ways the political conception of a nation." [20]

Nature can teach us this at any rate, that we must not expect to settle the problem of the universe on any basis of sheer individualism. We may argue as we will about the injustice of one being compelled to suffer for another. But it is the law of life, from the lowest grades of being upwards, and evasion of the fact is futile. The real point that concerns man is the spirit in which he will meet this enforced suffering for and through others. Whatever may be said about the animal world, which is certainly not tormented by questions of "rights" or moved to indict the justice of God, there is one clear answer to the "injustice" of vicarious suffering—that, as we move higher up the scale of human development, that which was resented as compulsion can be accepted as privilege, and that Jesus can set his face to go to Jerusalem, not in Stoic submission to an inexorable fate, but in the joy of a great purpose, to give His life a ransom for many. For such an attitude, the alleged injustice of vicarious suffering does not exist.

[20] From a review of Pasteur's work in *The Times,* Nov. 14, 1938.

4. What was the attitude of Jesus Himself to the world of Nature? We may assume that it was fundamentally that of the Old Testament. For Jesus the heavens continued to be God's throne and the earth His footstool.[21] For Him, the phenomena of Nature are the direct result of divine activity, unobscured by that elaborate net-work of second causes and of impersonal forces which exists for the modern mind. It is God who makes the sun to rise and the rain to fall,[22] who arrays the lilies of the field in their beauty and feeds the birds.[23] It is plain, from the Sermon on the Mount, that Jesus looks on Nature as an optimist, seeing in it a constant background of divine providence, beneficent in its operation. The miracle of the rain [24] brings fertility to the fields of the just and the unjust alike. Much of the suffering in human life which we should trace to natural causes was for Jesus due to the malignity of Satan and of demons [25] and belongs therefore to His view of human history rather than of the natural order. We may believe that when Jesus resorted to the solitude of the desert or of the mountains, it was not in the spirit of the ascetic John the Baptist, but because he found the ways of Nature

[21] Matt. V. 34, 35.
[22] Matt. V. 45.
[23] Matt. VI. 26-30.
[24] See Job V. 9ff. and Jer. XIV. 22.
[25] Luke XIII. 16; Matt. IX. 32 etc.

99

a true restorative; were they not to Him the direct
ways of His Father's providence, undisturbed by the
evil deeds of men or demons? Nor must we think of
Him as turning to Nature in the "romantic" reaction
from convention of the town-dweller, which charac-
terizes the holiday. Jesus was a realist in His attitude to
Nature.[26] The fact that Jesus used the *symbolism* of
Nature so constantly, e.g., the relation of the tree to
its fruit,[27] must not conceal from us the other and
more important fact that for Him Nature was *instrumental* to the providence of God. Thus the rising
of the sun on the good and the evil is not a symbol,
but an instrument, of the divine generosity which
forms the background of human experience. That
this generosity should be seen in the commonest and
most familiar things, such as the light and warmth of
each day, is significant; the religion of Jesus is that
of common life and is not meant to be the preroga-
tive of a minority, even though it may demand self-
sacrifice to a degree that seems attainable only by the
few. Within the framework of this universal beneficence, Jesus found room for God's individual dealing
with men. This is expressed, in Oriental hyperbole,
by the two sayings that "the very hairs of your head
are all numbered" and that the death of the most in-

[26] Cf. W. Schubart, *Das Weltbild Jesu* (1928), p. 29.
[27] Matt. VII. 16ff.

significant bird has significance for the God who has created and cares for it.[28] It is noticeable that, notwithstanding this particularism of providence, no place is given to contemporary beliefs in "fate", interwoven as they were with astrological beliefs. Sun and stars are no more than the instruments of God's large-hearted and personal generosity.[29]

This optimistic view of the general and particular providence of God must not, however, obscure the sharpness of the moral and therefore of the religious distinction which Jesus draws between the evil and the good, the just and the unjust. From the common beneficence of God in Nature, they equally profit; but the rain that brings life can also bring death, when its floods sweep away the house built on insecure foundations.[30] On the other hand, Jesus refers to the fall of a tower in Siloam which killed eighteen men [31] as a general warning and not a particular judgment; the sufferers were no worse than others. The truth of an individual retribution does not mean that it is exactly administered in this world, or that men are qualified to interpret it.

We may well believe that Jesus would have fully endorsed the Rabbinic contrast between the unfailing

[28] Matt. X. 29, 30.
[29] Cf. Schubart, *op. cit.*, p. 31.
[30] Matt. VII. 27.
[31] Luke XIII. 4, cf. John IX. 2.

obedience of Nature's ways and the disobedience of man's,[32] for this itself goes back to the teaching of the prophets. Did not Isaiah cry, "The ox knoweth his owner and the ass his master's crib: but Israel doth not know"? Jeremiah points out the similar obedience of the birds of heaven to their times and seasons in contrast with human "ignorance".[33] All this means that for prophet and rabbi and for Jesus Himself, the whole order of Nature is taken up into, and interpreted by, the personal relation of God to man, in which alone it becomes intelligible. But if that personal relation removes some of our difficulties, its higher level enforces new moral demands, and carries us forward from Nature to history.

[32] See, e.g., the passage quoted on p. 208 of *A Rabbinic Anthology* by C. G. Montefiore and H. Loewe.

[33] Is. I. 3, Jer. VIII. 7.

CHAPTER VII

PROVIDENCE AND HISTORY

A BRILLIANT French writer—Anatole France—with the gift of telling epigram, has offered us a summary of the history of men in three words: "born, suffered, died".[1] We may not be willing to accept the pessimistic view that the salient feature of the period between each man's beginning and end is suffering, but there is enough truth in it to give plausibility to the saying. When we contemplate the long succession of the human generations (short as the sum of them is by the measures of the universe), when we try to imagine, vain as is the attempt, the accumulated agony of the struggle to achieve a lasting satisfaction, with all its physical pains and spiritual anguish, all its broken bodies and baffled hopes, we may well admit that there is something here that demands explanation. In particular, what shall we make of the direct or indirect responsibility for this history which falls on Him who is credited with its creation and control?

[1] *"Ils naquirent, ils souffrirent, ils moururent."* Les Opinions de M. Jérôme Coignard, p. 200. The whole passage (from p. 197) should be read, to give the epigram its full force.

At the outset, we must, of course, affirm as unmistakably as possible that God is not directly responsible for that large measure of the suffering which springs from man's misuse of his own freedom, e.g., man's inhumanity to man. Whatever may be said of God's indirect responsibility for this, in the same sense as that a human father is indirectly responsible for the risks he may wisely allow his son to incur, risks for the boy himself and for others, it remains true that man himself has been and is the responsible agent for much of the actual suffering of history. This part of it is not our present concern. The moral gains of freedom in achievement and in character cannot be had without such risk of its abuse. If we believe that those gains are incomparably greater than those of any form of irresponsible existence which we can conceive, we have so far an adequate justification for God's gift of freedom to man. But the justification is admittedly partial, and still leaves much to be explained. Some of the data have already engaged our attention, since Nature, with her regularity, her dynamism and her corporate structure, is necessarily taken up into human history. For every group of men, there are racial characteristics and geographical conditions, with their physical factors of health or disease, and their climatic and economic consequences, which mark the limits within which human freedom operates. For any one generation or group, there will be the product of previous history in habits and institutions, prejudices and vested interests, which will produce a social inertia creating further limitations, as well as a dynamic of future movements. The social inheritance of bad laws, vicious customs and evil example is doubtless inextricably interwoven with wrong human choices. But it is not less inextricably linked with ignorance that might have been knowledge, with social relations that bring suffering on the innocent, with blind alleys of futile and wasted effort, that seem to deny any intelligent control of the course of history. Again and again, in the course of that history, might has triumphed over right, and injustice has called down no visible punishment of the evildoer and no visible vindication of wronged and suffering innocence. Whatever partial explanations we may be able to give of all these anomalies, one thing at least is clear—that "history is not self-explanatory".[2]

1. The field is immense and the records are fragmentary and casual, but certain aspects of it must impress us, even on so cursory a survey as can here be given. One of them is the slowness of progress, so far as it can be discerned at all, with all the resultant suffering of successive generations because of the lack of knowledge and power which might have been

[2] H. G. Wood, in *The Kingdom of God and History*, p. 7.

theirs. A book which had a wide circulation a generation or two back bears the title, *The Martyrdom of Man*. The author, Winwood Reade (nephew of the novelist, Charles Reade), thus explains the phrase:— "I give to universal history a strange but true title— *The Martyrdom of Man*. In each generation the human race has been tortured that their children might profit by their woes." [3] In support of his thesis, he divides the history of the world into four parts, viz., "War", "Religion", "Liberty", and "Intellect". The book is crude and often limited or erroneous in the information it gives, whilst it concludes with a violent and prejudiced attack on Christianity as hurtful in present forms to civilization. But it illustrates the kind of indictment of history that can be drawn up, as against the assumption of providential control.

It is undoubtedly true that the slow and painful course of history raises the same questions as does that of Nature. There is often, when we neglect the individual and think only of the mass movements of society, the same appearance of inevitability, the same suggestion of clumsy and creaking wheels along a heavy road, with obscure or wrong sign-posts. Statistics show a regular recurrence of conditions that would make economic laws as ruthless, *mutatis mutandis,* as those of "Nature"—in fact they are those

[3] P. 543 of the twenty-second edition; the first was published in 1872.

of Nature applied on the higher level of human life. The social history of man shows as little regard for the finer feelings of the individual as does Nature. Religion itself, when entering as it must the realms of social and political life through the organization which is necessary to it, becomes subject to the same controls. Even the motives and tendencies of human life, its fears and hopes, its loves and hates, show a deep kinship, a strange continuity, beneath all the varieties of their individual expression, so that man's boasted freedom and individuality seems often reduced to a minimum.

The cost of ignorance, in this long history, is not less than that of moral evil. We can hardly blame mankind for the fact that it had to wait until 1846 for Morton's successful administration of ether, and until 1847 for James Young Simpson to introduce the use of chloroform as an anaesthetic, and until 1864, for Joseph Lister to begin his work of antiseptic surgery in continuation of Pasteur's discoveries. But who can think of all the needless suffering and untimely deaths through all the previous generations without being moved to ask why the knowledge was withheld from them by the all-knowing ruler of the Universe?

In the realm of religion, at least, we might have expected such beneficent revelation as would have prevented man's ignorance from harming himself and his fellows. Yet we have only to think of the sufferings entailed by superstitions in all the ages, in order to realize that no such safe-guarding is visible. Witchcraft, with all the agonies inflicted by it on the innocent, has had in the past a universal dominion, and still prevails in the less civilized parts of the earth. "Suttee", the Indian practice of burning a living widow on the funeral pyre of her husband, was not made illegal until 1829, and cases have occurred in the present century. The Crusades, undertaken in the name of religion, left a long trail of immorality and suffering behind them, including the persecution and massacre of many Jews. The "Inquisition" of the Roman Catholic Church carries the ineffaceable memory of countless barbarities; who could stand, for example, in the old torture-chamber of Nuremberg, looking on its collection of ingenious instruments for the infliction of suffering in the name of Christ, without a shudder of horror, and some difficult questions as to what religion really is? They are living questions to-day, when new "religions" denouncing the old repeat the ancient story of persecution and cast down what had seemed securely established values, and when Nuremberg has acquired a new connotation.

What can we say about such things as these, of which history is so full, save that they are part of the price of human freedom and of the education of the race in the exercise of responsibility? But is it a sufficient answer? In the modern world, faced as we are by universal restlessness and anxiety, we are much less inclined to give an affirmative reply than were men of the nineteenth century. No doubt, the evils are brought home to us, as never before, by the extension and rapidity of our contemporary means of communication; no doubt, the increase of physical comfort on the one hand, and the loss of many stabilizing influences due to morality and religion on the other, have made us much more vulnerable to pessimism. We are hardly living in conditions to make a sound philosophy of history easy or possible. Perhaps only when a more stable political and economic equilibrium has been reached and the menace of war has been dispelled by saner methods of adjustment, will it be possible to pass a sound judgment on the meaning of history. We certainly cannot claim that history, as we see it to-day, demonstrates the divine providence. But we can, at least, remind ourselves of all those values of life which make it worth living, even whilst the fear of losing them increases our present anxieties. Our life has to be lived as part of a longer history, and we have no experience of any other world with which to compare it. We can see only that the possibility of our chief goods is bound up with that of our admitted evils, and that the race, like the individuals composing it, has (within certain limits not to be traced in advance) the power to increase the one and decrease the other. Mankind, as well as men, is on probation; until the issues of that probation are reached, we cannot pass any final judgment on divine providence in human history.

2. Another aspect of history which is difficult to reconcile with the providential control of it is the large element of apparent "chance", the significance for evil or for good of trivial incidents, mere accidents, irrational events in individual lives, fraught with the fortunes of an uncounted host of other men. When we say "chance" we mean naturally to imply a chain of causation which we cannot analyse; there is properly no such thing as "chance" in a world controlled by natural "law". But human lives and their relations to one another are far too complex for any complete analysis, so that "chance" conveniently describes something which we are unable to ascribe to any human purpose. How far does this element weaken our teleology and hinder us from seeing a divine purpose in history?

Mr John Buchan (now Lord Tweedsmuir) in his Rede Lecture at Cambridge in 1929, dealt with this theme under the title of "The Causal and the Casual in History". He reviews some of the principles which have been used in the interpretation of history and warns us against seeking any such complete causality as we find in the physical sciences—"All that we get are a number of causal suggestions, with a good many gaps in them". On the other hand he bids us make full allowance for those "momentous trifles" which we cannot rationalize, of which, amongst other instances, he names the fever which carried off the proper successor of James I in 1612, and the bullets fired in mistake by his own men which killed Stonewall Jackson.[4] His argument is meant to enforce humility in our claims to interpret history, and this applies whether we accept or reject the providential view of its course. But does the presence of what he calls the casual, as distinct from the causal, tell against the acceptance of that view? Not if we hold a large and enlightened conception of what such providential control must mean. It must not be taken to mean an occasional intervention in an otherwise fixed order. That is deism, not theism. Nor does it mean simply an immanent activity, working from below upwards towards an unknown goal. It implies transcendent purpose also, so that God works from above downwards as well as from below upwards. Something at least of this transcendence is implied in Jeremiah's words, "Am I a

[4] We may add an impressive example from another realm. The 1500 who perished in the sinking of the Titanic in 1912 would have been saved, it is said, if the ship had carried red danger rockets, for another ship was near enough, but disregarded the white rockets actually seen.

God at hand, saith the Lord, and not a God afar off?" [5] God is great enough to take into His purpose the little as well as the big, that which seems to us "casual" as well as that we are able to interpret as "causal", since for Him such differences do not exist. The warp that is stretched on the loom of the years is all one to Him, and the pattern woven by the flying shuttle of men's lives is taken up into that comprehensive pattern He is weaving, in ways beyond our comprehension. We may easily misinterpret this wholeness and unity of divine providence as we do God's dealings with the individual life, when we isolate particular events and treat them in isolation from the whole texture of life.

In both relations, those of national history and of individual fortunes, we may be too eager to look for "special providences" with the result that we impoverish life as a whole of God's controlling purpose and transforming power.[6] In the ultimate sense, the suffering that may befall a nation or an individual is God's will, even when it is not causally connected with discernible folly or sin. But we must not blame God for it, as though there were not a host of secondary causes, a network of Nature and history in which our life has to be lived. In regard to His con-

[5] XXIII. 23.
[6] See the remarks on this point in Ch. VIII.

trol of life, the casual ought not to present any greater difficulty than the causal, since the small things are not less in His hand than the great. The trivial event in history with its great consequences is paralleled by the trivial motives, the complexity of purposes in the inner world of the individual life, which have their great results in human decision and human destiny. Both worlds owe to God their creation and their conservation; shall He not say the last word as to their meaning? As I have written in another place, "All history is an ellipse, of which the land and the people are the two foci. . . . If we could write history as God sees it, the two foci of our ellipse would coalesce into the centre of a circle." [7]

3. Perhaps the greatest difficulty which history presents to the believer in divine providence is the suffering so often caused by the triumph of might over right, the successful tyranny of the evil-doer. It is not possible here to review the long succession of wars, massacres and persecution which history shows, nor is it necessary, since the modern world sufficiently illustrates the theme. Martineau's eloquent discussion of the subject [8] is well worth reading, even if we are not able to be quite as optimistic as he was about the intrinsic strength of goodness within the world to pre-

[7] *The History of Israel: Its Facts and Factors*, p. 11.
[8] *A Study of Religion*, Vol. II, pp. 109-130.

vail over its evil. That the suffering of the good may enrich the world with incomparable spiritual values is certainly true; whether and when it will change the evil wills of men to good is hardly within our power to discern, apart from our general faith in the ultimate victory of God. But we can see that suffering does bring out the true character of goodness, as Plato long ago discerned in regard to "justice". We can also see that one of the most powerful rebukes of moral evil is the spectacle of its consequences. If men really knew and reflected on the great demonstrations of this which history so amply provides, we might be living in a different world. But it would seem that each generation needs to learn the lesson afresh, and the "old, unhappy, far off things and battles long ago" must still find renewal to make their appeal and to bring their warning home to the consciences of men.

It does not seem, therefore, that we can demonstrate God's providence by an inductive process from the events of history, any more than we can demonstrate His existence by any of the familiar arguments for the being of God. We can meet intellectual objections and perhaps refute them by intellectual arguments. But we are left, most of us, with the consciousness that something is still wanting, some faith that can be used to interpret history rather than any conclusion that can be derived from it. In point of fact,

we still find that the ultimate reaction of the philosopher to the spectacle of human history always does
spring from the conditions of his approach to it.
Schopenhauer's classical presentation of pessimism is
at least as subjective as any of the varieties of Christian optimism. Whilst the philosophical form of that
pessimism was naturally drawn from the intellectual
conditions of his age, its tone and temper were derived from his own introspectiveness and melancholy
disposition. The ruthless and ineffective struggle of
"will" as the underlying reality of the universe was
notably the projection of his own temperament. But
the practical answer of mankind to any and every
form of pessimism is well expressed by Edgar's words
in the last scene of "King Lear":—

> "O our lives' sweetness!
> That we the pain of death would hourly die
> Rather than die at once!"

whilst even Milton's Belial expresses what is true for
the more reflective mind:—

> "who would lose,
> Though full of pain, this intellectual being,
> These thoughts that wander through eternity,
> To perish rather?"

The fundamental weakness of Schopenhauer's interpretation of history is, doubtless, the inherent incon-

sistency [9] of "unconscious will", which becomes in effect purposeless purpose. Just as Koheleth, "the Preacher" of the Bible, sees no purpose in the treadmill of life, because he has no sense of a redemptive past or a redeemed future, so does Schopenhauer compare man's history with the changing figures of the clouds, the eddies and foam-flakes of the brook, the frost-crystals on the window-pane.[10] With no purpose to redeem it from futility, there is little cause for surprise that man should seem to be tossed backwards and forwards between pain and ennui.[11] In sharpest contrast to this melancholy misreading of life stands the Biblical interpretation which centres in conscious and responsible volition, directed to an intelligent purpose. The Biblical references to "heart", which for the Hebrews was the psychical centre of "will", usually imply this. All through the Old Testament runs this conception of "purpose", as the key to life, divine and human, and the conception culminates in the teaching of Jesus and His own acceptance of the Father's will.

4. The previous chapter concluded by asking what was the attitude of Jesus to Nature. Here we may ask

[9] Cf. W. Windelband, *Die Geschichte der neueren Philosophie*, II, p. 367.

[10] *Die Welt als Wille und Vorstellung*, Bk. III, par. 35, E. T., *The World as Will and Idea*.

[11] *Ib.* IV. 57.

the parallel question—what was His attitude to history, including its spearpoint in contemporary politics?

At first sight, it is strange that Jesus makes so little reference to the history of Israel, as recorded in those Scriptures with which He was so familiar. We might have expected prophetic appeals to the deliverance from Egypt or prophetic warnings based on the sufferings of exile. As it is, the references are few— Jonah and Nineveh, Elijah, the Queen of Sheba, David and the shew-bread, the legislation of Moses.[12] Was it that the recorders of His teaching were looking forward and not backward? Or was He Himself so conscious of the crises of the hour, so insistent that no racial privilege could avail,[13] that He deliberately concentrated on the present? He assuredly felt that the time was fulfilled and that the kingly rule of God was at hand; [14] nothing mattered in comparison with this overwhelming fact.

In the interpretation of this characteristic emphasis, Jesus was no political revolutionary. Whatever He may have expected to happen to the Roman Empire in the new era, His answer about the tribute to Caesar implies clear detachment from political issues. The

[12] Luke XI. 30, 31, Mark II. 25, X. 3.
[13] John VIII. 39, cf. Matt. III. 9.
[14] Mark I. 15.

natural meaning of "Render unto Caesar the things that are Caesar's"[15] is that the political conditions under which the servant of God lives are relatively a matter of indifference; the implication is that of the Fourth Gospel, "My kingdom is not of this world".[16] There is also recorded His own payment of the temple-tax.[17] The unusual reference to Herod Antipas as "that fox"[18] is coupled with the declaration that political power cannot prevent His own religious mission.

In fulfilment of that mission it is plain that the sufferings of men are His direct concern, and that the power of Himself and His disciples to heal disease and exorcise demons is a central sign of the Kingdom, being indeed one of its constituent features.[19] Nothing could show more emphatically that Jesus regards suffering as an evil, to be expelled from the new order, than the fact that He ascribes so much of it to Satan and demonic powers. Nature, as God's creation, is not responsible for it; it is an intrusion into man's history and the cure of disease is part of the overthrow of the kingdom of Satan.[20] A large part of the Gospel narratives is the portrayal of human suffering and the rec-

[15] Mark XII. 17, Matt. XXII. 21, Luke XX. 25.
[16] John XVIII. 36.
[17] Matt. XVII. 24.
[18] Luke XIII. 32.
[19] Mark I. 34, etc., Matt. XI. 4, 5, Luke VII. 21, 22.
[20] Mark III. 22ff.

ord of the response of Jesus to it—a sufficient warrant, if one were needed, for our continuing to give a central place to social and medical service in the proclamation of the Gospel.

On the other hand, we must not take this healing ministry out of its setting. It belongs to the kingly rule of God, and entrance into that kingly rule requires repentance. "The Kingdom of God is within you." [21] Whatever victories over suffering be won by its removal, suffering will have to be endured by the members of the Kingdom so long as the present order lasts. That is most clearly expressed in the Beatitudes, where the blessing is closely linked with the suffering. Discipleship is itself a taking up of the cross. The disciple's primary purpose is not to escape suffering but to seek first the kingly rule of God. Then everything else will fall into its place, for it is God's business to carry out the divine purpose, with which the human has been linked. The kingly rule of God is in fact the *Weltbild*—the world-picture—of Jesus.[22]

It hardly belongs to our subject to discuss the vexed questions as to the incidence of the "Kingdom" of God, and how far Jesus conceived it as present or future. Both views seem to be present in His teaching,

[21] Luke XVII. 21. This rendering is preferable to "among you", in view of the antithesis of "observation".
[22] So Schubart, *op. cit.*, p. 53.

and however much we stress its "eternal" character, it is difficult to leave out that Jewish realism which demanded a visible fulfilment upon earth, whatever the heavenly significance of that fulfilment might be. Jesus assuredly contemplated a period of great suffering before the Kingdom came in its fulness,[23] and we can hardly think of the passing of that period of suffering into joy except as a visible and future vindication of God and the faithful. Exegesis and metaphysics must not be allowed to confuse each other, as they seem to do in some of the current references to "realized eschatology". But it is, of course, true that "each month is harvest-tide" [24] for the Kingdom of God.

[23] Luke XIX, 41ff.
[24] F. W. H. Myers' sonnet, "On a Window in Donington Church".

CHAPTER VIII

PROVIDENCE AND THE INDIVIDUAL

THE individuality of life is one of its most salient and striking features. Each human consciousness has a worth and colouring of its own. One of our novelists who has shown fullest sympathy with this aspect of life is Constance Holme. In her novel "The Lonely Plough" she is describing an elderly woman sitting by the fire in her cottage and strengthened by the thought that the end of life cannot be far away. This provokes the novelist's reflection—"*My* life!"—says every soul—"that sum of happenings which is mine and mine alone, that wonderful and dreadful pilgrimage that I have made with Time. Whatever the record, I have lived, finished the course, bound myself to Eternity by the tendrils of experience and growth". In the individual response to suffering there will be, of course, the greatest variety, if only because the capacity to feel, physically and mentally, varies so greatly in different individuals. There will also be the utmost variety of spiritual resource. One man or woman draws from wells of consolation which sim-

121

ply do not exist for another. One environment will
have hardened and strengthened the soul, if not rendered it callous, another may have softened it to the
point of defencelessness. This great variety, both in
the degree of suffering experienced and in the manifold reactions to it, must always gravely affect any
judgment we form on the mass of suffering in Nature
and history, seen from without. This variety of individual attitude will also affect the very important
factor of sympathetic suffering. Some people who
have lived selfish and self-enclosed lives are virtually
untouched by the sufferings of the multitude, except
so far as propinquity may affect their own comfort.
Others, gifted with keen imagination and a naturally
warm and loving heart, will suffer intensely through
the suffering of others, and will often be much more
conscious of these than of anything that befalls themselves.

It is only when we come to the individual experience of suffering that we can feel the full force of the
problem raised more abstractly by our consideration
of Nature and history. Let us take some definite examples of individual suffering in their concrete actuality. I purposely take four more or less ordinary instances personally encountered, of which the chief
merit as examples is that they are drawn from actual
life.

The first is that of an ex-science master whom I happened to meet in a friend's house. In the course of our conversation it emerged that he professed atheism, and finally he told me how this attitude to life began. In his early days, he had been a choir boy and he remembered very vividly one wet Sunday when he went to the church ill-clad and shivering, in shoes that did not keep out the water. At the church it happened to be part of his task to sing the anthem:— "This is the day which the Lord hath made, let us rejoice and be glad in it". He said to himself at the time "I don't believe it" and he told me that his unbelief in God clearly dated for him from that moment.

The second example is that of a doctor outwardly flourishing but inwardly embittered. In his student days he had been a Christian, finding time for Christian service amongst his university studies. "But," he said to me, "at the end of my course, I had to make a choice between two very different openings. I believed in prayer and therefore I prayed to be guided to the right choice. I acted in that faith and as a result of my choice all the troubles of my life have come to me. How can a man believe in providence after that?"

The third example is that of a nurse whom I came to know very well from her six weeks' ministry to me. She was a kindly, patient woman, approaching the end of her period of active service and looking forward to a time of rest after a strenuous life spent in the service of others. Not long after, I found her in hospital after an operation for cancer, confident of her convalescence. They had not told her that the operation proved that nothing could be done to save her, and the only mercy which providence seems to have had for her was in the anaesthetics which spared her something of the agony of the closing days.

The fourth example is that of a married couple, whom I had known from my childhood. They were both devoted Christians, giving time and energy and what they could afford out of a very small income to all manner of good works. Besides this, they impoverished themselves in the support of parents who lived to a great age. As the time of the compulsory retirement of the husband from his post drew near, financial anxiety so told upon him that he lost his reason. A few months after, his wife, who had looked after him herself with the utmost self-sacrifice so long as it was possible, lost her own reason, and had to follow her husband to the asylum where they both died.

I have given these examples just because of their homeliness, just because they are the kind of thing which all of us are likely to encounter. We may smile at the unscientific logic of the choir boy and the false diagnosis of the medical student, but even these can remind us of the individuality of the problem, whilst the two latter examples of physical and mental suffering admit of no explanation that would justify them as part of the providence of God. We ought to face this fact without shirking it if we are to say anything worth while about it. The suffering was entirely undeserved by any standard of human justice, and so far as could be seen, quite futile. As to the injustice, however, it is doubtful whether the individual is usually much concerned with his own rights over against the universe. That is an aspect of suffering which often impresses the spectator more than the sufferer himself, and something has already been said about it.[1] But it is the futility of so much suffering which is most overwhelming to the sufferer. "What good," he cries, "can it do to me or to anybody else that my body should be racked or my mind tortured like this?" Of course, it may often be true that the discipline of suffering has something to teach him, or that the patient endurance of the suffering might have a potent influence upon others. But such explanations hardly touch the third and fourth examples given above.

1. The simplest and most obvious reaction to suffering is that of the choir boy or the medical student —that of scepticism or agnosticism. Why go on try-

[1] See Ch. IV.

ing to believe in the dogma of a divine providence when personal experience so clearly contradicts it? Even if God's existence is not denied, there may be a weakening of faith in the care of God for the individual life. If we examine such a weakened faith more closely and intimately, we shall often find that it was bound up with a belief in "special providences" or the possibility of an infallible guidance. Now "special providences" are only too often claimed for trivialities, and a God of trivialities will soon become a trivial God. I remember hearing a lady in a Quaker meeting speak of her recovery of lost spectacles as a "special providence". She told us that she had found them at last by thinking of where she had been sitting—in the summer-house. God forbid that I should seem to doubt His concern with our individual interests, however small. But the psychical law of association is no more a "special providence" and no less a part of God's general providence, than the law of gravitation. There is something else that makes the term "special providences" a dangerous one, and one that often promotes unbelief rather than belief. This is that the believer who uses it too freely may come to think of himself as on terms of special favour with God, such favour as should exempt him from the suffering which other men must face. When such a belief as this meets with disappointment, as it sooner or later will, the faith that rested on it is only too apt to give way. But Jesus, in Gethsemane, asked for no "special providence" to exempt Him from His cross; His faith was able to make the instinctive prayer for help, with the true proviso, "if it be possible". That is always a real condition of Christian prayer, though it does not mean that it is wrong to pray for everything we need. We do well to remember Charles Kingsley's straightforward advice to some one who wrote to him about this question. "Pray," he said, "night and day, very quietly, like a little, weary child, for everything you want, in body as well as soul, the least thing as well as the greatest." Some of the great rules of prayer are given in those simple words: its regularity, its patience, its sense of the Fatherhood of God, its comprehensiveness, its relation to the actuality of life and its definiteness. The fact that we cannot translate our prayers into a complete scheme of divine providence ought not to worry us, and will not worry us if we have gained a sufficiently large vision of what providence is, if we have escaped from the provincial, indeed from the village, conception of God to the imperial conception. This ought not to mean to us that God is not concerned with the individual, but that the resources of His empire necessarily pass far beyond our ability to grasp them and that His fulfilment of our prayers will not be according to our own pattern and prescription. We have no right to stake our faith on a single issue, since we cannot know its full relation to all the other issues of life.

Much of what has been said applies to the other matter of infallible guidance, demanded by the medical student, which shall guarantee that we always know the right course to take. There is no such thing as infallible guidance for fallible men and women, and it is of no use to hanker after it, or to try to reduce it to a quasi-mechanical device. Higher religions move away from the sacred oracle, and as Dr Rufus Jones has somewhere said, there is no "supernatural click" to save us from the possibility of error, with all the disappointment or suffering it may bring. All we can do is to face the facts, frankly and fully, with all the intelligence God has given us, and with all the sensible advice which other men can give us. Then we can put the issue before God in prayer, and what our prayer will chiefly do for us is to test our own motives, and open the door in our hearts for the genuine guidance of God's Spirit. The misleading thing is often our inability to see the supernatural in the natural. God does not need to lurk in the chinks and crannies of His own creation. He can both guide and help us by means of the ordinary course of Nature and human life, and it is here that He should be chiefly sought. "Robinson Crusoe" tells us how tears of gratitude sprang to his eyes when he found a few ears of barley growing, as it seemed miraculously, on his desert island. But when at last he remembered that he had shaken out a bag of chickens' food just there, the wonder ceased, and with it his gratitude diminished. If, however, as Jesus did, we see God in all Nature and all history, we are the more likely to get clear guidance from Him when we are at a loss. Even so, this will never eliminate the risk of disappointment and suffering, which, for all we know, may be the very path in which God would have us go, the divine answer to our prayer which we fail to recognize.

2. In all this, we are acting on the great assumption of the Christian faith, that divine providence implies a personal relation between God and man. We are lifting our human life, with all its affairs, and all its setting of Nature and history, to the higher level of that personal relation to us. We are escaping from the false idea that the "miracle" must be a divine "intervention", a contradiction of the laws of Nature or of human nature. The regularities of Nature, so necessary for our mental training and moral development, are taken up into an unfettered personal control of them by God for our individual good, a control which can transform them or add to them, without necessarily annulling them.

One particular aspect of this personal relation to

God is that it inevitably introduces a new standard of values. This applies especially to the standards of motive. Is human life designed to provide pleasure or something greater, such as fellowship with a higher being? Obviously this question greatly affects our judgment of life. As Christians we shall say with Dr Tennant that "We cannot go behind our judgment, rational or non-rational, that the highest value in the hierarchy of values is moral worth or—what is the ultimate essence of all morality—personal love".[2] It may or may not be true that the order of this world provides the maximum of possible pleasure for the individuals belonging to it, but in any case that issue becomes irrelevant if once we are convinced that some things are of more importance than individual pleasure and self-satisfaction. We are then entitled to argue that the present world may be the potential door of entrance into a world above time, a world of eternal values not simply in quantity, but in quality. It makes all the difference to our judgment about any particular phase of our own individual life as seen from within whether we think of it as an end in itself or as leading on to something else. Thus the discipline of school or university cannot be judged properly without regard to the subsequent life for which it is intended to equip. Again, a man may pass through

[2] *Philosophical Theology*, II, p. 186.

some experience of great suffering from which he issues with greatly increased capacities to sympathize with others and to serve them.

These considerations lead up to the question of life beyond death. It is possible to make this no more than an escape from the problem of suffering, as when it is suggested that those who suffer greatly here may be amply compensated by their enjoyment of a hereafter. This is really a gross and materialistic way of handling the problem and is rightly resented by right-minded people. "Eternal life" is not an unlimited supply of the kind of life we have now and here. It is something different in quality, richer, finer, more spiritual. It is not to be regarded as compensation for the suffering which may enter into the present phase of experience, but as the fulfilment of spiritual capacities which could not have been brought into being without suffering. These two ways of looking at the life beyond death should be carefully distinguished, for they are really worlds apart. We might put the issue in another way by saying that no life is worth living here which is not spiritually independent of any life beyond death. That may seem a paradox, especially in view of the Apostle's words that if in this life only we have hope, then are we of all men most miserable. But those words had a special relation to particular circumstances and were bound up with a resurrection-faith in which quality and not quantity of life was the distinctive feature. Eternal life is in some degree a present possession of the believer. His experience of it is already intrinsically worth while and self-authenticating. However limited and fettered the present scope of that experience, however much the conditions of human life on earth, social and individual, may conflict with the conditions and realization of eternal life, yet the very essence of genuine Christian experience is that it does not depend on any extraneous rewards or justification. Within this personal relation to God, of which we already know something and into which the whole experience of the believer in God must be lifted, it is impossible to allow the issue to be settled by considerations which belong to a lower level of thought and experience.

That which has been said indicates one of the new elements, namely the new scale of values, which enter into the problem. Another element is that this personal relation to God of the individual believer springs from and is inseparable from the conviction of His triumphant love. In the light of a loving purpose the details of the individual life will be interpreted, but where no interpretation on that assumption seems possible, the conviction of the love of God will still remain as an effective practical answer to the apparent vagaries of providence. I cannot hope to understand fully what God is doing with me because His purpose necessarily passes beyond my comprehension. An engineer in India, during a cholera epidemic, found it necessary to fence in the wells and control the use of them by his native staff. It saved their lives, but they almost broke into revolt over it, saying, "Why should a man have to wait half an hour for water? Our fathers and our fathers' fathers never had to endure such oppression".[3] So we men often cry out against God, and misconstrue the purpose of a greater, wiser, more loving care. I am no more able to judge it finally than the little child can judge the purpose of its parents in the training of the home. All it can possibly do is to take for granted the love of mother and father when their conduct seems to lack any adequate explanation. Such an attitude is not credulity, it is based on the soundest principles of personal relation. No friendship would be conceivable if we did not credit our friend with a general benevolence of purpose passing far beyond any logical proof of it. The atmosphere of trust is just as necessary to the growth of personality as sunshine to the growth of the plant. That is true of human relations. It is also true of the divine. There will always be a residual mystery in the course of a human life considered as under the control of God. But in fact there could be no greater disproof

[3] Victor Bayley, *Nine-Fifteen from Victoria*, p. 154.

of divine providence than our own ability to explain *everything* in our experience—for that would bring God down to our own level.

3. Within the personal relation of God to the individual believer we have been dwelling chiefly on the divine activity. But we must not forget that His providential dealing with each of us is largely conditioned by the human activity which He has put in our power. This is seen not only in the general freedom of the human will and its moral responsibility for the right use of that real, though limited, freedom of choice, but very specially in the creative power inherent in man's constitution, to transform the meaning of events. This was mentioned at the close of the first chapter, where the claim was made that it was, in Wordsworth's phrase, "our human nature's highest dower". The more we consider this capacity, the more likely are we to agree that the phrase is no high-flown poetical extravagance, but describes a fundamental fact of our constitution, the importance of which cannot be exaggerated. We may instructively illustrate it by the important part played by chlorophyll in plant life. This is the substance that gives to plants and trees their green colour, and its function is to transform the elements derived from earth and air into the plant's food, when the plant is exposed to the sunlight. Since all animal life ulti-

mately depends on the food supplied by plants, we can understand the claim made by a distinguished biologist that chlorophyll is "the most wonderful substance in our world".[4] The statement deserves to be remembered in parallelism with that of Wordsworth. Just as the secret of all our physical life depends on this transforming power, which lifts chemistry to the higher level of biology, so we may say that the secret of all spiritual life lies in its power to transform every external happening into something beyond itself and so bring human life into its closest relation to God. There is no limit which we can assign to this spiritual power, which makes man a sharer in the creative work of God. It is an intrinsic and essential part of that spiritual consciousness which is God's gift to every man, and as such it precedes any attainment of religious faith, though such faith enormously increases the range of its powers. It enables the believer to re-interpret "the sundry and manifold changes of the world", and to discern in them, when viewed in sufficient range and with sufficient depth of insight, that purpose of God which is co-operating with his own in the shaping of his destiny. In particular, the challenge of all suffering, whether of body or mind, is robbed of the power to deny the providence of God, for the suffering can be transformed into

[4] Sir Arthur Shipley, in *Life*, p. 28.

some of those means of grace which have been already indicated. This is what is meant by saying that the religious fact is never the mere event, but always the event plus the religious man's reaction to it. That reaction is a unifying activity, which absorbs and assimilates the mere event, and derives new life from it, just as the plant can deal with carbon dioxide. This is why the Christian answer to the problem of suffering can never be reduced to a series of propositions. Any merely intellectual statement leaves out of account, or fails to do justice to, this capacity for spiritual transformation which is of the essence of the answer. Only from within itself does the Christian faith become fully intelligible and rational. Gradually do we discern the subordinate place of the mere happening, as compared with its *meaning* for the spiritual being whom it concerns. So we may come to believe that at the last the real fact is the meaning itself—the real fact in the spiritual realm. Perhaps all the interpretations of suffering that are valid are different applications of this ultimate truth.

But such a vision of ultimate meaning can never be complete for the finite spirit, living under the conditions of our present life. We see but the imperfect reflection of a metal mirror;[5] we do not yet know as we are known, in the fulness of the divine purpose

[5] I Cor. XIII. 12.

concerning us, which is the real meaning, and so the ultimate reality, of a human life. In present conditions of limited knowledge and discernment, there are certain to be features of our present experience which cannot be interpreted even in the light of all that has yet to be said about the love of God. That is true when we look out on the world of Nature and of history, as we did in the two previous chapters. It is still more true, when the individual experience of suffering comes into our view, as in this chapter. But it is just here, where the problem is most acute, where the "hard case" confutes our easy generalizations, that the resources of the human spirit, through the grace of Him who so constituted us, are most apparent. By virtue of this transforming power, men are constantly enabled to rise above their circumstances, and to give them a new meaning by which their worst elements are dominated. Such victories of the human spirit, as we have already seen, are not confined to religious faith—unless we hold that every loyalty to a larger spiritual or moral order is a form of religion, however imperfect in definition. But it is religious faith of the simplest kind which best enables the humble and lowly soul to win such victories.

We are entitled to claim, therefore, that there can be no solution of the problem of suffering which does not bring God Himself into it, and this not in the purely intellectual sense of a theism which would justify suffering, but in the practical way that God Himself shares in the suffering of the world He has created. After all, God is responsible directly or indirectly for all the suffering of which man is capable. Many men shrink from this conclusion and emphasize the large amount of evil brought into the world by man's evil will. This, as we have seen, is of an order different from the suffering caused through the working of the laws of Nature; yet, after all, it is indirectly the result of God's gift of moral freedom to men. God's creative responsibility, direct or indirect, seems to require that He should Himself help us to carry the burden of suffering. This brings us to the second main part of our subject, namely the suffering of God. Can God suffer? Does God suffer? How will His suffering help us in our own?

CHAPTER IX

THE SUFFERING OF GOD [1]

MEN have been tempted to think that philosophy moves ever on the same level in an endless circle, without ever reaching its centre, or even some height from which it can view the whole. Yet we may believe that there is a spiral ascent by which human thought, apparently traversing the same ground, again and again does reach higher levels and does move nearer to the heart of things.

The doctrine of God is one great example of this spiral movement. We shall see that the theology of the Bible from beginning to end is "anthropomorphic", in the sense that it speaks of God as though He were man, whilst continually reminding us, in its later stages, that He is more than man. We shall also see that when Biblical religion passed into a Greek world, all such statements were dismissed as merely metaphors, and God was assumed to be wholly free from human emotions, and defined in philosophic terminol-

[1] The subject of this chapter can never be made an easy one. Those who find the philosophical argument too technical for them can omit pp. 146-155.

ogy. Whilst this was the view of the Ancient Church in general,[2] modern theology has tended more and more to emphasize the "humanity" of God, His essential kinship with the human spirit which He has created. It is now much more widely admitted that the Biblical metaphors applied to God are more than metaphorical, and that they are the best expression of a truth about Him which has sound philosophical grounds. This is the argument of an important recent book, Dr Edwyn Bevan's *Symbolism and Belief*. He shows convincingly that the religious use of such terms as "heaven" above us, of the "glory" of God as light, of the "Spirit" of God as breath or wind, and of the "wrath" of God to express His attitude towards all that is evil, does not imply that they are "anthropomorphic" in the bad sense, but that they may have, and in fact, ought to have, metaphysical validity. They are symbols, but they are more than symbols. So we may come back to a higher anthropomorphism, of which we have no cause to be ashamed.

One cause of this change of outlook has been the re-discovery of the "Jesus of history", and the new emphasis on His humanity. The Christian conception of God necessarily centres in Him. This is not due

[2] On the whole subject, including the ancient forms of "Patripassianism", see J. K. Mozley's book, *The Impassibility of God*.

simply or chiefly to the fact that He was the historical founder of the new faith, as was Muhammad the
founder of Islam and Gautama the founder of Buddhism. Jesus occupies a place in Christian faith to
which there is no parallel in Islam's thought of its
prophet or in the original Buddhism, and He has oc-
cupied this place from the resurrection onwards. The
definition of that place has taken many forms, but in
general it has ascribed to Jesus Christ as the risen Lord
a relation to God that is unique. He is held to be not
simply the greatest of teachers, whose words about
God convey the most profound truth, or the doer of
mighty acts which witnessed to a unique human personality, but such a revelation of God that men could
believe the words ascribed to Him in the Fourth Gospel, "He who has seen me has seen the Father".

It is obvious, therefore, that the personality of
Jesus as known in the days of His flesh will profoundly influence the conception of God which we
derive from Him. However we conceive the relation
of the human to the divine in Him, His is at least the
kind of life that can reveal God. One of its outstand-
ing features is that it is a life of suffering in the years
that are known to us, and of a particular reaction to
that suffering. Whatever sunny years of silence may
have preceded the public ministry, whatever inner
joy and serenity sustained it, that ministry from first

to last was one of suffering, physical and spiritual.
Some phases of it and some incidents in it doubtless
brought joy to Him, but from the day of the temptation to that of the crucifixion, the quality of suffering was predominant. It was a life of poverty, of public scorn and private betrayal, of disappointed hopes
and misunderstood aspirations, which was crowned by
a shameful and agonizing death. It was, so far, a life
of failure, not simply by the standards of the world,
but by those of Jesus Himself: "O Jerusalem, Jerusalem, how often would I have gathered thy children
together!" There is a moment on the Cross when He
declares that God as well as man has forsaken Him. It
is not surprising that a little book which describes the
longing of an artist to paint a picture of "The Laughing Christ" (Pearson Choate) inspired by Franz Hals'
picture of "The Laughing Cavalier", finally leaves
the picture unpainted. When the mighty act of God
in the resurrection had reversed the natural verdict of
failure by the promise of a posthumous success, Christian faith had still to struggle with the paradox of a
suffering Saviour. The New Testament records some
of the early ways of overcoming it. Paul boldly declares that the apparent folly of the Cross is the veritable wisdom of God, who was working out a divine
righteousness through this death of His Son. The
Epistle to the Hebrews, with equal daring, converts

the suffering into a sacrifice and the sufferer into the Priest who offers it. The Fourth Gospel sees in the giving up of the Son to the death of the Cross the one adequate measure of the Father's love to the world of men.

In all this there is no direct transference of the sufferings of the Son to the Father, for the later problems of the doctrine of Christ's person and of the Holy Trinity are not yet on the horizon. But, on the other hand, it is assumed in the Bible (where volition is primary and intellect is secondary) that the personality of God is capable of emotion as well as of thought and will, the emotion of holy wrath as well as of holy love. The moral evil of the world moves God to anger, even though His love for men moves Him to costly sacrifice. In this the New Testament is true to the tradition of the Old Testament. God is indeed transcendent in Israel's fully developed conception of Him: "I am God and not man". Yet He is also a God who carries the burden of His people, knows the failure of His purpose for them, sorrows over them with a love that prevails over wrath, and in all their afflictions is Himself afflicted. When the Fourth Gospel [3] speaks of the divine Word as "tabernacling" with men, the association was "with the Divine tabernacle in the wilderness, when Jehovah

[3] I. 14.

pitched His tent among the shifting tents of His people, and shared even in their thirty-eight years of punishment".[4] This is the Hebrew thought of God, simple and direct and undeterred by those forbidding
words, "anthropomorphism" and "anthropopathism".
But when the faith that was born in a Semitic cradle
grew to manhood in a Greek world, when Christian
theologians began to shape the outlines of their own
religious faith, the tools that lay to their hands were
those fashioned in Greek workshops, and to Greek
ways of thinking about God their own thought had
to conform. One of these Greek ways was to conceive
God as "impassible", removed from any capacity to
suffer, indeed to feel, as men do.[5] It was taken for
granted by Christian theologians that the Biblical
ways of speaking about divine emotion were no more
than figures of speech.[6] As for the divine in Christ
which apparently shared His human suffering, a sharp
line came to be drawn between the human and the
divine natures. The suffering belonged to the human
side of Him, but not to the divine, for how could the
divine suffer? The result was that the Ancient Church

[4] Marcus Dods, in *The Expositor's Greek Testament, ad loc.*

[5] In Professor Edwyn Bevan's words, "Deity, every novice in Greek philosophy knew as an axiom, must be *apathēs*, without disturbing emotions of any
kind" (*Symbolism and Belief*, p. 210).

[6] "It is invariably assumed and repeatedly stated that impassibility is one
of the divine attributes." (G. L. Prestige, *God in Patristic Thought*, p. 6.
Cf. Mozley, *The Impassibility of God*, passim.)

in general could have no place for the doctrine of the suffering of God.

Only in the modern world, with its revived interest in the humanity of Jesus, and its reaction from what has seemed to many the artificiality of this kind of distinction between the human and the divine, has there been a return to the language of the Bible. From the suffering Christ, and with more or less explicit emphasis on the unity of His personality as seen in the earlier Gospels, men have looked up to a suffering Father. It has seemed to them monstrous to think of God as unmoved by the sufferings of humanity, for some of which He is responsible in having created them. It has seemed that the very Gospel of grace demands that love be enthroned at the centre of the universe, and they have professed themselves unable to conceive a genuine love that is not itself costly and sacrificial. No one has put the issue more forcibly than Horace Bushnell:—

"It is as if there were a cross unseen, standing on its undiscovered hill, far back in the ages, out of which were sounding always, just the same deep voice of suffering love and patience, that was heard by mortal ears from the sacred hill of Calvary." [7]

We may welcome the return to the doctrine of a suffering God as one inspired by a genuine religious

[7] *The Vicarious Sacrifice*, p. 31 (ed. 1866).

interest. But we must not accept it lightly or unthinkingly, without due regard to the real difficulties which attach to the conception. Theology cannot turn its back on philosophy without ultimate disaster. Let us consider, then, what these difficulties chiefly are, putting them, as far as is possible, in non-technical terms.

The most obvious of all objections to the ascription of suffering to God is that suffering in man usually means some kind of frustration or limitation. This may spring from our environment, as when a starving woman with her baby sits down in some African forest to die in the darkness.[8] It may be due to some malignant growth in the body which slowly destroys an essential organ. It may be wholly spiritual, as in the unforgettable bereavement. But in every instance it marks our finite nature and dependent position, and such suffering is irreconcilable with any valid meaning to be attached to the term "God". This objection seems particularly to hold in regard to suffering, for all kinds of "feeling", even more than thinking or willing, seem to be linked to the physical bodies which are part of ourselves; how can we conceive the feeling of a purely spiritual being? Altogether, it seems that the attribution of suffering to God is unworthy of Him.

Even if we say that divine suffering is, after all,

[8] An incident recorded in a Congo famine.

transient, something which God experiences as a necessary part of His purpose in creating and redeeming man, and that the final achievement of that purpose will bring Him perfect peace and joy, we seem to have entangled Him in the time-process, and to have conceived a changing God, moving like ourselves to something better. But religion instinctively demands the changeless as its fulcrum:—

> "Change and decay in all around I see;
> O thou who changest not, abide with me."

The time-element is indeed very closely interwoven with our human sense of suffering. As Professor Whitehead remarks, in a comment on the sun-dial inscription, *Pereunt et imputantur*, "The hours perish and are laid to account",—"Almost all pathos includes a reference to lapse of time".[9] How can a God exposed to such pathos be adequate to our religious needs, to say nothing of our philosophic speculation?

The philosophic difficulty becomes most acute when we are asked how we relate a suffering God to the Absolute. In ascribing suffering to God we are avowedly projecting human personality into God. All the general difficulties which attach to this projection affect the particular ascription of suffering to Him. Suffering makes Him relative to this or that part of

[9] *Symbolism*, p. 55.

His creation; how then can He be the Absolute, which philosophy has so often required, that all-comprehensive and self-existent Being, in whom and through whom all exists, and with whom alone the searching mind at last finds rest and consistency? Can God suffer without being less than the whole of things, a subordinate being who has vacated His throne in favour of the Absolute, or rather, has become One only, even if the greatest, amongst the appearances which have to be gathered up into some ultimate Reality?

These three difficulties—the apparent ascription of frustration, change, and limitation, to a God who suffers—are real, and negligible only by those who have not thought much about them. But an endeavour to meet them honestly can elucidate and enrich the idea of the divine suffering. In regard to the first point, viz., that suffering implies frustration, we must, of course, eliminate all thought of the suffering that springs from our physical bodies, since none of us supposes that God has a body like ours. Similarly, we can put aside the vast range of human suffering which belongs to moral evil, for the God of our faith is holy and righteous. Yet there remains in our experience the fact of spiritual suffering, arising from no bodily frustration, but voluntarily accepted for the highest ends. No man can seek to serve his fellows without bearing this burden. His disinterested activities will have selfish motives read into them. His attempt to arouse others to meet some practical need will encounter indifference or even opposition, where vested interests are attacked. In proportion as he rises above the average decency of others, he condemns himself to spiritual loneliness. What shall we say again of the suffering which springs from an intense sympathy with the sufferings of others, and is altogether escaped by the callous and brutal temperament? This moral suffering is something more than the mere *imagination* of the suffering of others, though that itself can bring anguish. The suffering of moral sympathy will be most acute in the most spiritually developed, those who are therefore most conscious of the

> "Desperate tides of the whole great world's anguish
> Forced thro' the channels of a single heart."

When to such sympathy there is added the strong purpose to go out and face the suffering involved in some great cause, when the philanthropist becomes the hero-martyr, we do not count it a frustration, but the richest fulfilment of life. But if the will to suffer vicariously can so enrich human personality, why should it be considered *in itself* to be a frustration of the divine, if on other grounds divine suffering is held to be conceivable?

The adequate answer to any difficulty that remains

149

is naturally that of the self-limitation of God, His free acceptance of suffering to which in Himself He is not liable. If He is held to suffer automatically, and not of free choice, then He is indeed a limited and frustrated God, struggling with an alien environment. This would apply, of course, if the material world were not of His creation and He were gradually enforcing His will upon it, to reduce it to order. It would apply, also, if rebellious spirits in the seen or unseen world had so broken away from His control that He was powerless to do anything but wage war with them, something after the manner of Milton's "Paradise Lost". But neither applies, if God is the world-creator and the world-redeemer, voluntarily limiting Himself to a gradual creation of cosmos out of chaos, and to a redemption of rebels by grace, instead of an annihilation of them by force. Now this is precisely the Christian conception of God and of His purpose. So far as it involves suffering for Him, it is an enrichment of that purpose, not its frustration.

But this brings us to the threshold of the second difficulty, which is indeed the greatest of all, that of the entanglement of God in the time-process. This must not be minimized, for it is the fundamental problem for philosophy, and therefore for philosophical theology. To discuss it adequately would require a volume, and when that volume was written, it would be but one more in a row of many like it, reaching back to the beginnings of man's intellectual effort to interpret the universe. But it is relatively easy to see where the paths diverge, and to recognize the choice which we have to make. Is Time at last no more than a shadow cast by Eternity? Are we really content to say with Henry Vaughan?—

> "I saw Eternity the other night
> Like a great *Ring* of pure and endless light,
> All calm, as it was bright,
> And round beneath it, Time in hours, days, years
>   Driv'n by the spheres
> Like a vast shadow mov'd, in which the world
> And all her train were hurl'd."

No one can doubt that that way of looking at life has its genuine religious value. But is it an adequate statement of our experience, and of the pre-suppositions of that experience? If Time were only shadow, without substance, if all our striving, our laughter and our tears, our temptations and our sins, our loves and our hates, were known to be illusory, in spite of their *apparent* reality, could it remain for us what we all in fact accept it to be—something of serious worth to ourselves, something to cling to, even to the last, something in which our choice of good and evil is indeed our own, and carries its own burden of responsibility? Take from a man the deep-set conviction that life means something, and something of supreme importance, and you have paralysed all his higher purposes and activities. But if this life in time does mean something to man, it must mean something to God, who made him and it. Just what it means to God can be expressed only in the language of time, and the expression is necessarily symbolic. But this does not necessarily mean that what is expressed is not more than a symbol. It may be—it must be, unless we are all victims of illusion—not so much a symbol of reality as a part of it. Time is then the most valuable of all our possessions, though it is that of which we are most careless. Time is with us from birth to death, yet its definition is one of the most difficult problems of philosophy. Time may be so related to Eternity that it registers something from moment to moment which already has eternal significance and does not even depend on the final issue for its only value and worth to God. The time-process, as well as the time-result, may concern Him, in His own great way, as much as it concerns us. It will be the path of His chosen purpose, which includes just this creation of spirits with their limited but real freedom of choice, and with all the possibilities of happiness and suffering, of joy and sorrow, which we know to be ours. As a part of that purpose, there must be a sense in which it *adds* something to God's universe, though it can add nothing to God Himself, save the manifestation of His grace, in the creation and development of spirits which can have fellowship with Himself. If that is worth while for God, as it seems worth while for man, then we may believe that God's acceptance of the burden of the whole time-process, with all that its sin must mean to His holiness, and its suffering to His sympathy, is worth while to Him, though it be at the cost of much suffering. Doubtless, it is easier to conceive a static than a dynamic God, philosophically easier to detach Him from the suffering of the world than to involve Him in it. But we may fairly ask whether the Gospel of the divine purpose can be derived from a static God at all. In that purpose we see the unchanging will of God, and in that sense He is the unchanging One. But the changes which are involved in the working-out of that purpose, the changes which make the very actuality of our human life, may be conceived as the utterance of the purpose itself in a richer language than that of the intellect. Traherne is putting this point when he says of God, "When all that could be wrought by the use of His own liberty was attained, by man's liberty He attained more".[10] The cost of that "more" to Him is something which we can but call "suffering", but it is suffering so taken up into His eternal purpose as to be

[10] *Centuries of Meditations*, IV, 46.

transformed into joy, for we know that the suffering even of a man, for noble ends, can be so transformed.

But if God's relation to the world is conceived in the way indicated, does it not commit us to a God who is less than what philosophy calls the Absolute? Does He not become One amongst the many, instead of being the One and only source of the many? Canon Mozley is surely right when he insists on an answer to this question before we are free to assert that God suffers. Indeed, it is the same question as we have had before, though in a new aspect. The dilemma is that if we identify God with the Absolute, we leave no room for the religious values already indicated, whilst if we bring God within the Absolute He becomes too small a God, not only for philosophy, but also for religion. We must set God in the highest place, if He is to remain God, and that means that He must be identified with the Absolute, when we are working with philosophical terms. God must be ultimate, in the sense that nothing beyond Himself is necessary to account for Him and for the world in which He is manifested. But if the religious values of our experience are to be justified, we must so relate the world to God as to make its apparent reality part of the ultimate being of God. If it be said that any "relation" of the world to the Absolute, the unrelated, is a contradiction in terms, the natural conclusion is that the fault is in the use of the term Absolute at all, and that we must be content to assert that God corresponds with the philosophic Absolute in being the one and only and all-comprehensive source of all being, but that His being is itself seen in such a continuous outflow of creative activity as is exemplified in our world.[11] This is another way of saying again that time is in God, and not God in time. Our religious vocabulary must necessarily continue to address God and speak of Him as if He were in time, if not also in space. But even whilst we use such ways of speech, and conserve the realities they represent,[12] we ought not to forget what is involved in saying that God is also the source of all that is, and that without Him it would not be. This also has its religious value, even though it be expressed in quasi-spatial metaphor, just as "divine purpose" is itself a quasi-temporal metaphor, though, as Pringle-Pattison suggests, purpose comes nearest of all our conceptions to express the nature of the eternal.[13]

But we have been fighting a rear-guard action against certain types of philosophy long enough. Let

[11] Cf. A. E. Taylor, art. "Theism", in the *Encyclopaedia of Religion and Ethics*, Vol. XII, p. 261: "From a theistic point of view it is, no doubt, proper to call God, the being from whom all others are derived, the Absolute or unconditioned being, but only on the condition that the Absolute is not equated with all that really exists."

[12] On this point, see Professor Edwyn Bevan's Gifford Lectures, *Symbolism and Belief* (1938).

[13] *The Idea of God*, p. 358.

us wheel and attack the doctrine of divine impassibility by asking what meaning there can be in a love
which is not costly to the lover? We measure love by
its degree of sacrifice; apart from the cost, it would
be but idle sentiment. The Christian Gospel of the
love of God owes all its power of appeal to the manifested grace of Christ, a grace seen in the cost of
love. We are not here concerned with the varying
ways of interpreting the costly offering of the Cross,
but with the simple fact that the constraining love of
Christ is seen in history as a costly love. Just so far as
we take the great leap of the Christian faith, and
ascribe such love to God Himself, do we seem compelled to say that for God also, love is costly, involving suffering. One evasion of this inference is found
in the resort to the Chalcedonian doctrine of two distinct natures in Christ. His costly love is then rele-
gated to the human nature, whilst the divine does
not suffer at all. This is the usual method adopted by
orthodox theology when it denies suffering in God.[14]
Jesus Christ by His human nature shares in the suffering of man, but by His divine nature in the un-
mixed joy of God. This is not the place to discuss the
adequacy of such a Christology. The presentation of

[14] As by von Hügel, in *Essays and Addresses* 2nd. Series, p. 209: "He has
allowed real, direct Suffering to come as close to Him, in the humanity of
Christ, as, in the nature of things, Suffering could come."

Jesus in the Synoptic Gospels gives no evidence of such a cleavage. It may be sufficient here to urge that if the divine nature has simply appropriated that which cost the human nature so much, we have no warrant for saying that "God so loved the world". The giving of His Son upon the Cross cost Him nothing in suffering, and the human love is greater than the divine. Here we may notice with interest a Rabbinical argument against the divine Sonship of Jesus. It is urged that if God could not bear to see Abraham sacrifice his son, He would not have looked on calmly whilst His own Son was slain.[15] The argument, of course, is futile against those who believe that He did not look on calmly, but suffered in and with His Son, accepting the suffering as His way and His Son's way of Saviourhood. But it does remind us that we cannot have it both ways. The more we appeal to the love of Christ for man, in life and in death, as revealing the love of the Father, the more we seem driven to ascribe the sacrificial quality of that love, its very essence and core, to the Father as well as to the Son. We ought to be able to understand the indignation of a modern theologian:—"Theology has no falser idea than that of the impassibility of God".[16]

We do not reach the characteristic Gospel of the

15 J. H. Hertz, *The Pentateuch and Haftorahs*, p. 923.
16 A. M. Fairbairn, *The Place of Christ in Modern Theology*, p. 483.

Christian faith until we see the glory of God in the face of Jesus Christ, until we are brought to affirm that in Calvary God is commending His own costly love towards us. Apart from this truth, Calvary would not have dominated history; it would have remained an obscure, perhaps unrecorded event. The terrible sufferings of crucifixion do not explain the centrality of Calvary, for countless others have suffered such physical agonies and are forgotten. The innocence of the sufferer will not explain it; again a countless host might have written on their graves the inscription on that of a French convict, afterwards found to be innocent, who died in the 23rd year of captivity:—"Here lies Vaux: he has gone to ask justice of God".[17] Nor is it enough to dwell on the manner of Christ's death—that He bore His sufferings with the courage and patience of a hero. That alone would simply put Him with Stephen, and with Socrates. The uniqueness of the Cross lies in what it achieves in the redemption of man, and that achievement is bound up with the costly love of God. The human *love* of Jesus was necessary as the effective language of the divine; is not the human *cost* inseparable from the love? But if this be true, is not that human cost part of the revelation of the divine cost of love in suffer-

[17] P. 277 of H. B. Irving's *Last Studies in Criminology*, where the case is described at length.

ing? Make every allowance for the difference of the eternal from the temporal; confess that none of our human language is adequate (which applies as much to "love" as to "suffering"); recognize that sorrow and suffering cannot be the last word or the dominant note for God; we are still left with the need for something in God that will correspond with the suffering of holy love in man, something that justifies our faith in God and His forgiving love when we look upon the Cross of Christ.

If we seek further confirmation of the suffering of God, we may find it through the doctrine of the Holy Spirit. The work of the Spirit, we are taught in the New Testament, continues and completes that of Christ. We may say, indeed that there is a second Incarnation, not confined to a single life, but extending through all the generations. The Incarnation of the Holy Spirit has the same marks of God's ways. It is a *kenosis*, a self-emptying, like that of the Son which Paul describes in Phil. II. It involves the acceptance of the lowliest conditions—how else can we think of the Holy Spirit indwelling such men as we are? It marks indeed a lowlier descent than that of the Son. For Jesus was the sinless among the sinful; in His consciousness there was no evil to grieve the Holy Spirit, and man's sin could but beat upon Him from without. But if we take seriously the doctrine of God's indwelling of the believer through the Holy Spirit, then God accepts a deeper humiliation, for who of us is sinless? Such an intimate association of Himself with us cannot mean anything but continual suffering for God, even though it is a suffering transfused with the joy of sanctifying the sinful. This is recognized in the New Testament, where we hear of God as Holy Spirit being grieved by our sin,[18] insulted by wilful relapse,[19] teaching our infant lips to cry, Abba, and witnessing with our spirit that we are God's children,[20] helping our weakness and making intercession for us.[21] All these are lowly offices, as truly as that of washing the disciples' feet. They mean that the Spirit also has taken on Him the form of a servant, a suffering Servant. If that does not mean the suffering of God, then our whole Christian experience is based on an illusion. For that experience builds on the truth that we have to do, as directly as the time-process permits, with God Himself, God as known through "the Spirit of the Lord". We may, then, confidently accept the statement of such a theologian as Horace Bushnell when he says that the Spirit:—

"has His Gethsemane . . . if the sacrifices of the much-enduring, agonizing Spirit were acted before the senses in

[18] Eph. IV. 30.
[19] Heb. X. 29.
[20] Rom. VIII. 15f.
[21] V. 26.

the manner of the incarnate life of Jesus, He would seem to make the world itself a kind of Calvary from age to age." [22]

We may add the words of a philosopher—Pringle-Pattison—who ranks high in his understanding of the essential Christian truths, when he says, "if God is not thus active in the time-process, bearing with His creatures the whole stress and pain of it, the immanence of the Creative Spirit becomes an unmeaning phrase".[23]

The fuller significance of the doctrine of the suffering of God will engage our attention in the two following chapters. But its profound effect on any doctrine of the atonement is obvious. The redemption wrought by Christ in sacrificial and costly suffering on earth will have its great analogue in the eternal realm, and every suggestion that the Son placates an angry Father will be swept away. We shall have to consider whether some worthier conception of atonement is not necessary to replace this "transactional" theory. In the posthumous volume of sermons by H. R. Mackintosh, there is one on the text, "He that spared not His own Son, but delivered Him up for us all, how shall He not with Him also freely give us all things?" The preacher reminds us that everything in Christianity goes back to the self-sacrifice of God,

[22] *The Vicarious Sacrifice*, pp. 43, 47.
[23] In *The Spirit*, ed. by B. H. Streeter, p. 18.

that the Cross is a window into the Divine heart, and then goes on to say some pregnant words about what is often called "the mystery of the Atonement":—

"We say, truly enough, that it is difficult to comprehend how forgiveness comes through the work and suffering of Christ, and how what went on at Calvary avails to save us. And often by our very manner of saying this, a suggestion is left that the difficulties are purely intellectual. If we were abler, if our minds were more subtle or profound, it is hinted, we should not find the Cross so unfathomable as we do. But doesn't the difficulty lie far, far deeper? I feel that the great reason why we fail to understand Calvary is not merely that we are not profound enough, it is that we are not good enough. It is because we are such strangers to sacrifice that God's sacrifice leaves us bewildered. It is because we love so little that His love is mysterious. We have never forgiven anybody at such a cost as His. We have never taken the initiative in putting a quarrel right with His kind of unreserved willingness to suffer. It is our unlikeness to God that hangs as an obscuring screen impeding our view, and we see the Atonement so often through the frosted glass of our own lovelessness." [24]

[24] *Sermons*, pp. 176, 177. For the theology behind this sermon, see *The Christian Experience of Forgiveness*, by H. R. Mackintosh (Nisbet, 1927).

CHAPTER X

REDEMPTION BY DIVINE SUFFERING

IN THE previous chapter it was maintained that there is no valid philosophical or theological objection against the doctrine that God suffers, and that the genuinely Christian conception of God in fact requires that, in some sense, He should be a suffering God. It was claimed that such a God was revealed both by the human life of Jesus Christ, and by the continued indwelling of the Holy Spirit in the fellowship of the Church and in the hearts of its members. On this basis, the present chapter will examine in what sense the divine suffering is redemptive.

The best-known of all accounts in the extra-Biblical literature of what the Cross does for the sinner is that of Bunyan. The pilgrim comes "to a place somewhat ascending; and upon that place stood a Cross, and a little below, in the bottom, a Sepulchre. So I saw in my dream, that just as Christian came up with the Cross his burden loosed from off his shoulders, and fell from off his back, and began to tumble, and so continued to do, till it came to the mouth of the

Sepulchre, where it fell in, and I saw it no more". That is the often-quoted account of an experience; here from "Grace Abounding" is the less familiar doctrine implicit in that experience:—

"One day, as I was passing into the field, and that, too, with some dashes on my conscience, fearing lest yet all was not right, suddenly this sentence fell upon my soul, Thy righteousness is in heaven. And methought withal I saw, with the eyes of my soul, Jesus Christ at God's right hand. There, I say, was my righteousness; so that wherever I was, or whatever I was doing, God could not say of me, He wants my righteousness, for that was just before Him."

There we have doctrine, and of a very definite type —that of the Protestant Reformation; the doctrine is inseparable from the particular form of experience which Bunyan has given to his pilgrim.

On the other hand, we must not fail to recognize that there may be a reaction to the Cross quite comparable with Bunyan's, a reaction which rests on and implies a very different type of doctrine. Such was St Teresa's, when kneeling before a crucifix, she was overcome with the sense of her own unworthiness. "She felt she never had anything to offer God, nor to sacrifice for His sake. The Crucified One consoled her by saying that He gave her for her own, all the pains and labours that He had borne in His Passion, that

REDEMPTION BY DIVINE SUFFERING

she might offer them to His Father." Implicit in that
experience is the doctrine of the Mass, the Catholic
doctrine of atonement by sacrifice over against the
Protestant doctrine of justification by faith. Yet both
Catholic nun and Puritan tinker kneel together at
the foot of the Cross, reconciled to God through it.
The experience, therefore, of reconciliation to God
through the Cross is wider than any particular doctrine of it, whilst never separable from *some* form of
doctrine.

Each particular doctrine claims to be an interpretation of the events, and springs from the experience
of the Christian that in and through the Cross he is
actually reconciled to God. The events in themselves
can be regarded simply as part of human history. The
way that led from Galilee in the north to Jerusalem
in the south, the path from the Upper Room down
into the Kidron valley, and up the slopes of Olivet to
Gethsemane, and then by way of a traitor's kiss, and
a high priest's prejudice and a procurator's pusilla-
nimity to Golgotha—all this is perfectly natural and
explicable as a series of human events. The actual suffering of the Cross, its agony of body and soul, the
blood that streamed from the nailed hands and feet,
the pathetic cry of dereliction—this can arouse our
pity or our indignation, but not constitute the ground
of our faith. Even the prayer that the executioners

might be forgiven, which wins our moral admiration, was echoed by the first martyr. In fact, as Pascal says, in his disconcerting way, Luke has portrayed a stronger death for Stephen than for Christ (though Pascal adds that Christ's trouble came from within, not from without). How then can events which, in themselves, simply move us to pity or indignation or admiration create the experience of reconciliation to God which we know men have so often found before that Cross? The answer clearly lies in their interpretation—the interpretation of faith. Because of the Person of the sufferer, not because of the magnitude or intensity of the suffering, men have been brought to the intuitive conviction, which no verbal argument can compel, that this suffering is, in some sense, the suffering of God, that Christ's attitude towards it, of willing acceptance and transforming forgiveness, is the attitude of God, and that something has been done here on Calvary that concerns every sinner and God Himself.

This is the point at which emerges the distinction between the so-called "subjective" and "objective" doctrines of the Atonement. On the one hand, there is the view generally popular to-day which makes the redemption to consist essentially in a revelation of God's love, changing the attitude of the sinner; on the other, the view which fully admits this truth, but also sees in the work of Christ a redemption which has objective meaning and value for God Himself— so that the revelation consists essentially in a redemption, rather than the redemption in a revelation. The distinction can, of course, be pressed unfairly against either type of doctrine. The "subjective" or "moral influence" type can be represented as if it took the emphasis off the objective work of grace in making the revelation, the "objective" type as if it were necessarily a mere "transaction" between Christ and God which virtually robs God of the grace of His saving purpose. We must avoid both tendencies, for on either view it is asserted that "God commendeth His own love toward us, in that while we were yet sinners Christ died for us", and on either view the penitent return of the sinner to God is included. The real point to decide is whether the suffering of Christ has a Godward, as well as a manward reference, whether there is something in the very nature of sin, the sin of the race and of the individual, which requires God to do more than to declare and reveal His forgiving love.

Now, it is significant that the main trend of doctrine through the Christian centuries has been to assert the "objective" view in one form or another. This is not the place to attempt any comprehensive survey of the varieties of doctrine which have done this. It is sufficient to recall the characteristic view of the

Greek Church that Jesus Christ, by His life and death and resurrection "actually" brought the divine attribute of immortality into the world of mortal men and so made men partakers of the divine nature; that the Western Church, from the time of Augustine onwards, regarded Christ's death as a ransom paid to the devil, purchasing the deliverance of sinful men from his power; that Anselm taught the Church to conceive of Christ's death as a "satisfaction" of the wronged honour of God; that the Reformers emphasized the conception of a penalty due to sin, which was suffered by Christ in place of guilty sinners. In more recent times the essence of Christ's work has been seen in some form of representation of man, the vicarious offering of e.g., a perfect penitence which was beyond the powers of man. Whatever we may think of any or of all these attempts to interpret the sufferings of Christ and the actual experience of reconciliation to God through Him, they do provide a powerful testimony to the existence of a felt need— that God must do something for man, which he cannot do for himself, before the declaration of divine forgiveness can become effective and convincing.

In general, these theories are the expansions of metaphors, more or less adequate, which break down when they are worked out logically, or force us to conclusions which we are unwilling to accept. Does our present line of approach through human and divine suffering enable us to do justice to this objectivity without entanglement in particular metaphors?

In the first place, as has been repeatedly emphasized in this book, Jesus won an actual victory over moral evil by the transformation of the crime into the glory of the Cross. He overthrew sin, not by enlisting against it material forces, or even "twelve legions of angels", but by allowing it to do its worst and then transforming this worst into His best. The evil was permitted to triumph over the good that the evil might show its own nature and its utter futility when matched with the good. The Cross was a focal point of victory wrought by the goodness of Jesus against the evil of the world, though at a spiritual cost which we cannot measure.

In the second place, this actual victory in time can be interpreted as the downward extension of that victory wrought in eternity by the suffering God over the sin of the whole world, the victory by a transformation of the consequences of sin into the occasion of holy grace. The temporal victory is just as much God's as the eternal, though it is achieved in a human nature which partly disguises its ultimate significance from us. How that downward extension of the divine in the Person of Christ was brought about we cannot fully comprehend—but how could we expect to stand outside God and humanity, which is what "comprehension" would require? Standing on the earth and looking up to the Cross, we see a suffering Man, yet one who shows Himself more than man by the very quality of His suffering and of His victory over it.

This victory of Christ is not simply *symbolic* of the hidden victory of God; by being that part of the divine victory which we are permitted to see it becomes the supreme victory, the *instrumental* centre of historical redemption. It is a temporal event, but it is also part of the eternal reality which the Gospel proclaims. So far as history means anything at all to God, this is actually and positively His central victory within it. The victory will not, indeed, be complete until individual men have laid hold of the hem of God's garment as it hangs down on Calvary and felt the saving virtue of His power transform their sinfulness into spiritual health and give them victory over evil. All through time, where their sin abounds, grace does more abound. The sin of the world is like the waves of an angry sea breaking on the eternal shore, and transformed from its sullen darkness into the gleaming beauty of the breakers. The divine grace, which is the divine will to forgive and to suffer in forgiving, does not only defeat sin, but makes its consequences contribute to the spiritual beauty of the universe.

God, like His Son, does not wait for man's penitence to be gracious, though He may have to wait (as the Old Testament puts it)[1] before He can show His grace. It is the grace of His forgiveness that moves men to a true repentance and it is this actual "redemption" of evil by its transformation into good which constitutes, in its historical counterpart, the Christian revelation. It is wrought by God for man, whether on earth or in heaven; but it is also wrought by God *in* Himself, since it springs from His own nature, and must be a victory of *grace,* and *for* Himself, since the sinful history of the human race is His intimate concern. Sin is an intruder into God's universe, but the "iridescent" wisdom of God [2] has made around that intruder the pearl of grace.[3]

On this view, then, the Godward relation of the historical atonement will be that it actualizes in time the eternal reality of God's saving purpose, not only by actually bringing man to penitence, but also by actually transforming the *values* of history. The Cross shows the actual and undeniable transformation of the evil wrought by the crucifiers into the occasion of

---

[1] Is. XXX. 18.

[2] Eph. III. 10 (*polupoikilos sophia*).

[3] I have dealt with some of the questions that naturally arise for such a view of redemption in the essay, "The Christian Gospel of Redemption", in the volume called *The Christian Faith* (ed. by W. R. Matthews). I hope to return to the subject on a larger scale in a book on *Redemption and Revelation.*

grace, and warrants the personal faith in each of us that God can transform the consequences of *my* sin also into the opportunity for His grace. I shall still sorrow over that sin, past and present and future, but it will be with the godly sorrow which knows that it cannot be separated from the love of God which is in Christ Jesus. The faith on which I rest is that God is able by His grace to transform all evil into good, whether past, present or future. I see Him doing it on Calvary, and so far as I am really penitent, I feel Him doing it in my own heart, and I trust Him to do it on the vast scale of His universe. I accept the inevitable retribution of sin as not only just but merciful, because disciplinary. I can freely use the great metaphors of atonement, such as sacrifice, satisfaction, penalty, representation, whilst knowing they are only imperfect metaphors, to express certain aspects of the actuality of grace. Jesus offered Himself to God for me, Jesus did for God's honour what I ought to have done and failed to do. Jesus suffered from the consequences of sin as though He had been one of us sinners; He suffered as I deserve to suffer. Jesus represents me in the presence of God, and I am made one with Him by the union of faith. But the defect of all these metaphors, *when they are made the starting-point of a theory of atonement,* is that they are too external. They represent God as a potentate who needs a gift before he will hear me, or a feudal lord whom I have offended, or a judge in the rather stuffy atmosphere of a law-court, or as someone rather inaccessible who is unwilling to grant me a personal interview.

We must get closer to God, in order to know the truth about His grace. The name Jesus used, "Father", brings us closer, but is itself a metaphor, and has been over-worked, either as the basis of theory, or as the excuse for its absence. To-day, with modern associations, it is apt to hide the divine authority and the sterner aspects of God's inevitabilities as it did not in the ancient world. Our primary need is to find the essence of atonement, as well as the necessity for it, in the very nature of God. The atonement then shows itself, not as an ancient transaction in an Eastern land, but as an ever-continuing law of God's own nature, containing the infinite promise of a new creation through transforming grace. The objectivity of the Cross is seen in the actuality of its transformation of evil, that transformation being the final proof and substance of forgiveness, the actuality of time transformed into the pattern of eternity. We are often reminded by men of science that the universe is not a permanent structure, that, like ourselves, it is born to die, and that the only "progress" it displays is "progress to the grave".[4] But the Cross of Christ shows us that the order of the spiritual world reverses that of the physical. It moves not from life to death, but from death to life. Our interpretation of its ways and means must change, and must go on changing, for we cannot cease thinking. But in the grave by the Cross, where science ends, and faith begins, the pilgrim still buries the burden of his sin, to go on his way rejoicing, in the strength of the new life of fellowship with God, through Jesus Christ.

In what has so far been said, we have been keeping as close as possible to the Christian experience of forgiveness, though we have also noticed the necessary implications of "doctrine". We have been endeavouring to find an "objective" redemption through such a transformation of evil into good as was actually wrought out on the historic Cross of Christ. The suggestion has been made, though not developed, that this transformation was the earthly counterpart of a divine and eternal reality. Can we make that suggestion more definite and more convincing, even at the cost of some repetition?

Consider, first, why sin needs more than a divine edict of forgiveness, powerfully proclaimed by the

[4] Sir James Jeans, *The Stars in their Courses*, p. 152.

Cross. If we hold with Abelard and Rashdall that the Cross of Christ simply *reveals* the love of God, and so moves the sinner to repentance, without any other Godward significance, we are not likely to have so profound an experience of sin and forgiveness as had Bunyan and St Teresa, who both held that the Cross achieved something essential for God as well as for man. If there is something more in divine forgiveness than the simple acceptance of human penitence, it will be because penitence does not exhaust the consequences of sin. If we know what doctrine of sin is held by a theologian, we know, in general outline, the kind of doctrine of the Atonement he will hold. Rashdall, for example, has very little to say about sin; that explains why he is content to believe that Abelard was right and Anselm was wrong. To all who hold Rashdall's view,[5] Anselm still puts his cogent objection to the statement that sin is destroyed *sola compunctione*—by repentance alone:—*"Nondum considerasti quanti ponderis sit peccatum"*. "Not yet hast thou considered how great is the burden of sin." When Anselm goes on to say that a single look contrary to the will of God ought not to be purchased by the values of a whole world, most men would describe it as an exaggeration; yet I think Anselm would have the Preacher of the Sermon on the Mount with

[5] E.g., R. S. Franks, *The Atonement* (1934).

him. There is something in the character of moral evil which makes it incomparable with anything else. If it be done in ignorance, it is still a defeat of God's purpose; if it be done in knowledge, it is a defiance of His will. Whatever its history, however entangled with natural passions or social customs, it has acquired *actuality*, for which the sinner remains responsible. We cannot shake off that responsibility by any disavowal of it; the very nature of human personality, which incorporates into itself the whole of its own past and is nothing if not continuous, should teach us that there is no "Statute of Limitations" in regard to sin, as there is none in regard to crime. The evil act is as irrevocable as the good, and its irrevocability extends to countless other lives, as well as to our own. No right-minded man will ever forgive himself for his own wrong-doing; ought he to believe that the holy God can dismiss sin more lightly than he does himself? If our good concerns God, does not our evil? If God's purpose is to be worked out in a time-series of events as the product of free agents, does not the partial defeat of that purpose by sin concern God, and concern Him in regard to the process, as well as to its final outcome? How has God dealt with that which has passed beyond human control—the sinful record of human history, social and individual? Must its pages be forever defaced by the ugly blots which man's hand cannot erase? If human life means anything real at all, its evil meaning is not less serious in the eyes of God than its good. Time is not eternity, but in some real sense, time is a part of eternity and God cannot be content simply to ignore the sinful past of one man or of the whole race, and simply to say "I forgive you".

The first step then of our argument has been to urge that the actuality of sin still concerns God, and this, even supposing that the sinner repents of it. The next step is to consider what must be the relation of this actualized sin to holiness in God. There is an ontological question to be faced before we reach the soteriological one. Time, as we have seen, is in God, not God in time. In some sense, all the time-agents and all the actuality of the time-series, whether good or evil, must live and move and have their being in God. We may relieve Him of the direct responsibility for the actuality of sin by the doctrine of His self-limitation through the creation of free spiritual agents. But they are upheld as well as created; they would cease to be, if He were not upholding them in their doing of good or evil. What place, then, has this actual evil within the creative and conserving activity of God which is the constant expression of His nature?

In saying "what place", we have already committed

ourselves to a spatial metaphor, inadequate as it is. Let us boldly use it for what it is worth, whilst admitting the inadequacy. Imagine God as the great all-comprehensive circle of Being. For the theist there can be nothing outside that circle. Within it there are smaller circles representing spiritual beings, such as man, with the gift of free creative power. If they were all to use that power in perfect harmony with the will of God, they would become concentric circles with God's centre as their own. But with one exception all of them are self-centred, in differing degrees of remoteness from the divine centre. Within each of those circles there is something alien to the quality of the all-comprehensive circle, which is holiness. Holiness cannot endure the existence of sin within itself; yet each of these smaller contained circles itself contains the actuality of sin. The only way in which we can resolve that paradox seems to be this—that *the actuality we call sin is existent within God only as suffering.* As sin it can have no existence within Him, but because it is alien to His purpose, though permitted by His will, it becomes for Him suffering. If it be said that this is philosophical speculation rather than Christian theology, let us consider the reaction of *human* holiness to sin. If we give holiness its full content of Christian meaning, holiness cannot be mere withdrawal from sin; it must include,

178

among other things, the suffering that evil inevitably inflicts on its opposite good. Just as a vulgarity of manners hurts a man of good taste, just as coarse and ungrammatical speech jars on the educated ear, so in a far more important realm, moral evil inflicts pain on moral good; in fact, the only way in which moral evil can enter into the consciousness of the morally good is as suffering. If a good man is brought up against some dastardly act like David's treatment of Uriah, he will not simply repel it, he will inevitably suffer from the very experience of it; it hurt Nathan to be brought into contact with it, and out of such suffering came his sympathetic parable of the ewe lamb. It hurts good men even to think of such things; how much more to live with them! But how much more still, beyond our imagining, to be responsible for their continued existence, as is God! Is not our sin His suffering, because of our relation to Him and His to us? Let us put aside all thought of suffering on God's part as an arbitrary device. Let us think of it as just as inevitable in its own supreme order as the suffering of the good through the evil in our social solidarities of earth. Few things are more necessary in theology than the elimination of the arbitrary. God is not arbitrary in physical nature; there we see Him working by law and order. Will He be arbitrary in the more important world of things spiritual? Will

179

not the Atonement, if it be found to involve the suffering of God, present itself to us not only as an event of history, which God has turned to good account, but as something that springs from His own nature, and *is* inevitably, because He is what He is?

As we have seen,[6] the suffering of God will not spring, as does most of ours, from the imperfection or the limitation or the inconsistency of His nature. It will be the suffering that springs from moral, not from physical necessity, the suffering of holiness, choosing to suffer, such suffering as we see in Jesus. To ascribe such suffering to God is not to dishonour, but to honour Him, for:—

> "this is the authentic sign and seal
> Of Godship, that it ever waxes glad,
> And more glad, until gladness blossoms, bursts
> Into a rage to suffer for mankind." [7]

Such thoughts as these have already brought us another step on our way, the important step from suffering in itself, to suffering as "grace". It is evident that one reaction of the divine holiness must be retributive, since the evil-doer is setting himself against the purpose of the holy God.[8] That is certainly a part of the truth in the relation of sin and holiness, though it belongs to the realm of the Law and has not reached

[6] Ch. IX.
[7] R. Browning, *Balaustion's Adventure*.
[8] See Ch. V.

the level of the Gospel. We are mistaken, when we think of forgiveness chiefly as the remission of penalty. The essential penalty of moral evil, in a universe controlled by a holy God, is intrinsic and inevitable, and therefore not to be removed by any formal remission. It does not depend on the social sanctions of human life, which often fail to correspond with the divine sanctions, by their excess or defect. The retribution that awaits, or rather, that accompanies, sin, has nothing arbitrary about it, either in its infliction or its remission. As Emerson put it, "Crime and punishment grow out of one stem. Punishment is a fruit that unsuspected ripens within the flower of the pleasure which concealed it." [9] In that respect, there is no fault to be found with the underlying principle of the penal or retributive doctrines of the Atonement. Their fault is not that they say too much, but that they say too little. They do not sufficiently represent the inner inevitability of penalty; they do not sufficiently express the intrinsic quality of grace, as the most characteristic reaction of the divine holiness. Perfect holiness, either in man or God, cannot be content with retribution; it must exercise the "necessity" of grace springing from its own nature. Grace is not the antithesis to holiness, but its finest and fullest expression.

[9] Essay on "Compensation".

So far, we have thought of sin as having a two-fold consequence—as inevitably involving retribution for the sinner, and not less inevitably suffering for God. Now suffering in itself has no moral value; it is, so to speak, so much raw material of life. We cannot say what suffering means to a spiritual being till we know what will be his attitude towards it. It may make a man better or worse, as we say; but that will depend entirely on what he himself does with it. It may sweeten his nature or it may embitter it, according to his own reaction to it. Similarly, though *mutatis mutandis,* the suffering of God will derive its significance from His attitude to it. That attitude might have been one simply of holy retribution to the cause of the suffering, but if it had been that, and nothing more, we should never have had the Christian conception of God. The characteristic feature of that conception is grace, and grace here means the *voluntary* acceptance of the suffering in the working out of the divine purpose to save. Does that seem a contradiction to what has been said already about the inevitability of the suffering of holiness in God? If it does, this is because we are forgetting that there is no before and after with God, and that His purposes spring from His nature, and that His choice includes all the links in the chain of its own accomplishment. God suffers because He is holy, and God accepts the suffering because He is holy, and God saves through the suffering because He is holy. Given the God and Father of Jesus, grace is morally inevitable, because it shares in the spontaneity of His whole purpose. God is not passive, but active, and active in perfect holiness throughout. The suffering due to man for his sin is taken up into the purpose of grace, and penalty becomes vicarious suffering. There is a transformation of meaning, and meanings are the only ultimate facts in the spiritual order. No activity of spirit, human or divine, is more remarkable than this power to give new meanings to events, as we have already seen.[10] If that is true of man at his best, how much more true must it be of God, working in the high realm of a necessity that is not physical but moral! In that high realm, His saving purpose transforms His suffering into a more glorious expression of His own nature. So, in a wider sense than Paul's reference to the Jewish Law, "where sin abounded, grace does much more abound". In all this we are speaking, not simply of events on earth, but of the eternal purpose that controls them. Except for the events, we should not have known the purpose, but the purpose, the eternal purpose, exists independently of the events. God has always been transforming the fact of sin by His own attitude towards the suffering which it occasioned in

[10] See Ch. I, end.

Him. We are here accepting the principle rightly affirmed by Professor H. R. Mackintosh, that "whatever constitutes the central core of atonement must be predicable of God; you must be able to carry it back to God Himself and say—What Christ felt, did, suffered, was in the truest sense felt, done, suffered by God. For the atonement really is the cost to God of forgiveness".[11]

[11] *Some Aspects of Christian Belief*, p. 93. Bushnell's second volume, *Forgiveness and Law*, has some interesting points of contact with this, but suffers from his attempt to put new wine into old bottles, and to cling to categories which will not serve his purpose.

CHAPTER XI

THE FELLOWSHIP OF SUFFERING, HUMAN AND DIVINE

WE HAVE been thinking, in the previous chapter, of divine suffering as redemptive. If this principle be accepted, does it throw any light on the sufferings of the whole costly process in human history, to which the suffering of Nature is a prelude and accompaniment? Can we, with this crowning fact of divine suffering in mind, recognize a purpose in the process which will help to justify the suffering in it beyond anything yet said?

We can best begin by frank recognition of the limitations of the previous arguments about human suffering. The incompleteness of the explanations given on successive levels has been repeatedly admitted. The Bible itself gives not one, but several explanations of suffering, both in the Old Testament and in the New, and not even the sum of them all provides a complete answer to our questions about the purpose of suffering. In the Bible, it is sometimes represented as the just retribution for sin; at other times it is explained as the discipline or "chastening" of individual character. In social relations, it may have the character of witness-bearing to a truth held by the sufferer, or it may even be interpreted (in some unexplained way) as having the quality of an offering or "sacrifice" made to God, or a penalty borne vicariously.

But in spite of all that has been said, we are left with a vast amount of suffering, in Nature, history and the individual lives of men, which seems sheer waste or cruel torture. Nature indeed appears to achieve particular ends by this expensive process, such as the evolution of distinct species by natural selection (which means the unrestrained conflict of life with life for bare existence). But what is the good of the whole process or of the whole result? If it goes no further, if it produces nothing beyond itself, is all this pain justifiable, on any theory of divine control? If we point to man, as the supreme product of this long travail, we are again forced to put the same question on the new level of self-conscious life, with all its intensifications of the problem and most of all the emergence of moral evil. Our answer might well be that if there is no movement to something beyond, the world is, in Rabindranath Tagore's striking phrase, "a prison-house of orphaned facts".[1]

[1] *Personality*, p. 61.

Even if we share the Christian faith that there is a richer and fuller life beyond death to which man may attain, this is but a partial answer to our questions. Some of the individual suffering in this world may indeed be a necessary preparation for another and better one—but how often this explanation of suffering seems to break down! We see men and women whose suffering is protracted far beyond the point at which it might plausibly be represented as useful either to themselves or others. We see the aged, or little children, deprived of those on whom they would naturally lean, just when their service is most needed. We see human fellowships broken off, not when their mission has been fulfilled, but just when they are but the promise and potency of years to come. It is as certain as anything can be that no adequate theodicy can be constructed for the individual lives of men within the present horizon, even when we have fully allowed for the transformation of meaning wrought in the sufferer himself.

This failure to reach an adequate solution of the incidence of suffering in the individual life is just what we might have expected, if the argument of Ch. IV, "The Individual and the Society", is sound. We must resolutely refuse to make difficulties out of abstractions, and it is an abstraction to isolate the individual from the society to which he belongs, and without which he could not be. This is brought out by the place and value of human sympathy with suffering. Fundamentally, sympathy [2] is an instinctive feeling, which we share with others, just because of the physical and mental bases of our social solidarity. It is quite unreflective at this stage, as may be seen in the contagion of crowd-consciousness, which may sweep the individual will along with it. There is, of course, no moral value in "sympathy" at this stage, though the capacity for it, and the imagination which increases it, are natural endowments which can become of great value under moral direction. The comfort brought to the sufferer by human sympathy, apart from any practical service that can be rendered to him, seems to spring from the re-affirmation of the social ties, from which his suffering has temporarily isolated him. We all know how helpless we feel in regard to saying anything adequate in the presence of great suffering. But we may usefully remember that silent sympathy is often its most eloquent and effective form of utterance. The look, the hand-clasp, the manifest concern, —these often say the essential thing better than words can. That essential thing is to remind him in the isolation induced by pain and suffering that he still be-

[2] There is a good article on "Sympathy" by Sophie Bryant, in the *Encyclopaedia of Religion and Ethics*, XII. See, also, the moving incident in Miss Helen Waddell's *"Peter Abelard"*, p. 103.

longs to a larger social order. Perhaps this is always the first step in the upward path leading to the discovery of the love of God. We might adapt a familiar word of Scripture and say, "If a man be not loved by his brother whom he hath seen, how can he know that he is loved by God whom he has not seen?"

We have seen that we cannot be members of a society without being called to suffer through our relation to others. But does the recognition of this fact bring sufficient help in the explanation of suffering? It brings some—for one of the most harassing elements in suffering is its wastefulness and futility, and the sting of suffering is removed when its utility for a worthy end can be shown. The hardships of the pioneer and the discoverer, the risks of medical research, the loneliness and spiritual travail of the prophet which bring some new truth into the world, the agony of the martyr who witnesses to it, the wearisome nights and days of the nurse and the mother, the toil and disappointments of the teacher or pastor—all these and countless other forms of suffering find their sufficient explanation in the progress of the individual or the race. Healthy-minded men and women do not really complain that such burdens are thrust upon them, for in their hearts they count them as privilege and opportunity. But what of the long-drawn-out agony of an incurable disease from which nothing

189

can be hoped either for the sufferer or for others? It does not seem a sufficient answer to say that pity and sympathy may be awakened and that service to the sufferer can itself be a spiritual training. That is true, so far as it goes, but it does not go nearly far enough to meet all our difficulties.

Suppose, now, that our problem of human suffering is lifted to a new level, by being related to the suffering of God. That suffering construed through the visible suffering of Christ has been seen to have a redemptive value. Can the suffering of those who are linked to Christ by faith be so related to what He has done as to supply a new source of explanation of the mystery, not excluding the partial explanations offered on lower levels of life, but gathering them up into something higher and more satisfying? This, at any rate, has been the belief of many of Christ's disciples, since the days of the Apostle Paul. Everyone remembers that great saying of his, "I rejoice in my sufferings for your sake, and fill up on my part that which is lacking of the afflictions of Christ in my flesh for His body's sake, which is the Church".[3] Different views have been held as to the precise meaning of these words, but it seems safest to say that they point to the Apostle's sense of mystical union with Christ, "the fellowship of His sufferings" which he else-

[3] Col. I. 24.

where [4] couples with "the power of His resurrection" as part of the highest Christian experience. It has been well said that for Paul, suffering becomes "the third sacrament".[5] We must not confine such sufferings to those which are incurred directly through "taking up the cross", in the path of Christian obedience. For life, or at least the Christian life, is a unity, and all its experience is brought within the scope of its dominant purpose. Thus Paul's "stake in the flesh" [6] is accepted by him as part of the divine providence that encompassed his life; it was a messenger of Satan made by God to serve the useful purpose of inculcating humility and showing more effectively the power of Christ in him. This warrants the Christian in regarding all his suffering, from whatsoever source it comes, as part of the cross which he is called to bear in the service of God.

Now, there can be no question here of any suggestion that the redemptive work of God actualized on Calvary is incomplete, or that Jesus is simply *primus inter pares*. The redemptive suffering of Christ is unique, supreme and fully adequate because of His unique relation to God. But that relation of believers to Him which incorporates them into His Body—the relation of faith—also commits them to be willing

[4] Phil. III. 10.
[5] H. Windisch, in *Die Religion in Geschichte und Gegenwart*, III, col. 1564.
[6] II Cor. XII. 7.

cross-bearers with Him. This principle, as the one essential element of discipleship, was emphatically expressed by Jesus Himself, when He said, "If any man would come after me, let him deny himself, and take up his cross, and follow me"; [7] and again, when He tested those who sought a high place with Him in the hereafter, "Can ye drink the cup that I drink?" [8] There is no place at the heavenly banquet, or at the table of the Lord on earth, for those who are not willing to drink of the cup of Gethsemane. The same truth is not less emphatically expressed by the Apostle Paul, when he says, "I have been crucified with Christ".[9] But he goes on in the next verse to disclaim any "righteousness through the law", which would "make void the grace of God". It is clear that he does not think, here or elsewhere, of his own sufferings as having any independent merit before God. They are, as we have seen, the suffering of Christ in him, because Christ lives in him. In this sense, and in this sense alone, these sufferings fill up that which is lacking.

But such a fellowship of suffering with Christ and with all who belong to His mystical body surely lifts all suffering potentially to a new plane, and gives it a

[7] Mark VIII. 34, and compare William Penn's *No Cross, No Crown.*
[8] Mark X. 38.
[9] Gal. II. 20.

new meaning. So far as the sufferer shares the purpose of God, he becomes a creative fellow-worker with Him in the continuation of that redemptive work which was initiated on Calvary. When the martyr Stephen dies, praying for those who are killing him, "Lord, lay not this sin to their charge" he is drawn into the closest fellowship with Christ on Calvary, praying, "Father, forgive them, for they know not what they do". The attitude to the suffering is the same in both, whatever difference there be in personality. Stephen's, indeed, is derivative and Christ's is primary. But if we find a value for God in the human sufferings of Jesus, we must not refuse to see it in those of Stephen, in their own degree and order. Protestant prejudice against the doctrine of the "merit" of the saints ought not to operate here. We do not rob Christ of His unique glory in the work of man's redemption, if we find that the redemptive principle revealed in Him is operative also in all who belong to Him, that in fact it is still His work in them. We *must* find some such intrinsic principle, something that springs from the nature of things and is universal in operation, if we are to remove the artificiality of so many doctrines of atonement. We have found it in the suffering of God which transforms all that is evil into good by making it the occasion of grace—the willingness to suffer. Shall we hesitate, then, to say that all the suf-

fering of a believer in Christ is potentially the material waiting transformation through the Spirit of
Christ in the believer?

Nor ought we to draw an absolute line at conscious
faith in Christ, so far as this principle of fellowship
in suffering is concerned. If Francis of Assisi stands
out as one who pre-eminently reflects this glory of
the Lord in the Christian centuries, what shall we say
of Jeremiah as a forerunner of Christ, suffering with
God and for God? He did not indeed reach the full
graciousness of forgiving his persecutors, but he accepted, with many an inward struggle that reveals
the cost, the suffering for himself which, he declared
to Baruch, was experienced by God.[10] Seeing that God
girds men for their task when they know it not [11] we
must ascribe to His "prevenient grace" all true endurance of suffering and not exclude this from the
working out of His whole purpose for the world.
Have not the great sufferers, such as Socrates, outside
the line of closest revelation, also something to contribute by their suffering to the ultimate transformation of the world's evil to good?

It is not easy to urge this principle as a possible interpretation of all human suffering without seeming
on the one hand to minimize the redemptive work of

[10] Jer. XLV. 4 and cf. Jeremiah's teacher, Hosea (Hos. XI. 8).
[11] Is. XLV. 5.

Calvary and on the other to exalt suffering as itself
redemptive, apart from the attitude of the sufferer
towards it. Needless to say, neither conclusion is here
intended. The difficulty of statement is inherent. In
regard to the former, the difficulty springs from the
fact that no man can separate the work of God in
himself from the contribution of his own will. In
Christian experience, all is God's and all is man's: we
work out our own salvation, though with fear and
trembling, because it is God who works in us both to
will and to work for His good pleasure.[12] So, on the
higher level still, and further removed from any analysis of ours, there is the distinction between the work
of Christ's humanity and the divine work in and
through it. What difference for our eyes can there be
at that level between the perfection of our humanity
in Him and the grace of the Incarnation, the Word
become flesh?

In regard to the possible objection that the argument tends to regard suffering as a good instead of an
evil, we must re-emphasize that it is the *transformation* of suffering that is in question, not suffering in
itself. Everything will depend on the attitude of the
sufferer and what he does with the raw material given
him to shape. But if he shapes it aright, he will know
something of the joy of the sculptor wrestling with

[12] Philipp. II. 12, 13.

the recalcitrant block of marble, or of the poet struggling to bring an inadequate and clumsy vocabulary
into the service of his vision. The artist's achievement
essentially consists in this overcoming; apart from it
he is a dreamer of dreams, whose beauty can but rebuke him. So it is the challenge of suffering that calls
us to transform it from all its ugliness into the thing
of beauty which it becomes as an offering to God. It
is the act of offering which is the transforming touch,
but if there were nothing to transform, the beauty
could not be.

Something of this thought underlies the argument
in James Hinton's classic, *The Mystery of Pain*
(1866), the book which von Hügel made his starting-
point in a notable discussion of *Suffering and God*.[13]
Hinton's book is rather untidy in arrangement and
his thought is not as clearly expressed as it might be,
but the deep sympathy with suffering and the strong
conviction that it is not purposeless explain its continued appeal. He sees that the pain of suffering can
be swallowed up in joy, when love transforms the
suffering into sacrifice, and he is convinced that an
unseen work is done by us, though we cannot see the
ways in which God is using our suffering. Nor does he
shrink from believing that God suffers. But he fails to
bring together adequately the suffering of God and of

13 See the bibliography at end of this book.

man, perhaps because he hesitates to impinge on the
redemptive work of Christ. Moreover he avowedly
leaves the fact of sin out of the reckoning. But no discussion of suffering ought to do that. We cannot so
isolate innocent from guilty suffering, because we are
all bound together in the unity of society. We cannot
even isolate our own innocence from our guilt, even
though we recognize that some of our sufferings come
as our own "fault" and others through the "fault" of
the society to which we belong or of the Nature amid
which we originate. In the solidarity of society we
are all bound together, for evil as for good, and all
that lies in our power is to decide whether that enforced solidarity shall become by our choice a willing
fellowship. That fellowship will not be with man
alone, for we are bound up in the bundle of life with
the Lord our God.[14] We see Him using the transforming work of His Son—"made perfect through suffering"—to initiate us into a like privilege, that we
may share with Jesus something of the joy of the
Cross. Because of the uniqueness of His relation to the
Father, which makes of His suffering the perfect
achievement in time of an eternal reality, we cannot
think of our suffering as "merit" that avails for our
own or for others' redemption. We cannot put the
solidarity of the race as crudely as does the Rabbinic

[14] I Sam. XXV. 29.

parable which says that God looks on the mingled
Israelites, good and evil and those betwixt and between, and says, since it is not possible to destroy
them, "Bind all together into one bundle and the one
will atone for the other".[15] The Christian cannot put
it as crudely as that; yet surely beneath the crudity
there is a truth, the truth of a willing fellowship of
suffering with God, glad to suffer in the achievement
of His redemptive purpose. If He who says "Be ye
holy, as I am holy" has called us into the holy fellowship of His grace towards sin by His Son our Saviour,
can He not give us a humble share in the redemptive
suffering of transforming grace wherein His Son is
the first-born among many brethren? God does not
ask more than He wills to share.

If that be true, our human history acquires a new
meaning. It is no longer the record of a questionable
progress to the dubious goal of human perfection, under the shadow of a slow fading out of life or a cata-
clysmic end to it—a goal which even if achievable
would still leave unanswered the problem of the suffering of countless generations which have been but
scaffolding to the building of the last generation of
all. History now becomes the record of man's privilege
to share, by his very sufferings, in the redemptive
work of God, through which even the record of his-

[15] *A Rabbinic Anthology*, Montefiore and Loewe, p. 229.

tory with all its sin and shame may be transformed into the record of God's grace. We must indeed go on working for the betterment of man on earth, physical and moral and spiritual. That is both the test and the means of the inner growth into fellowship with God. But that fellowship is a present fact and the eternal can be as real to us now as it will ever be. The temporal is seen to be not the symbol but the instrument of the eternal. By its means we can rise to the truly spiritual level of a fellowship with God in which all suffering may become worth while for His saints and even for lesser men, as most of us are. If, in the final retrospect of spiritually enlightened eyes, all past suffering is seen to have contributed to the divine glory in the redemption of the world, then the final verdict on history will be like the initial verdict on Nature, "behold, it was very good".

I asked a Christian man, who had suffered through many years with little or no hope of escape from the physical pain, what his suffering meant to him. He thought a little and then said, "Well, it seems as if one came up against a blank wall, with no way through, and then—a door opens." I said, "And what is the key that opens the door?" "Ah," he replied, "God has the key of that." A good answer, for all our attempted explanations of the mystery can but bring us at last to cast ourselves on the love of God, and to find our answer in fellowship with Him who suffers with us and for us. The simple test of our real knowledge of that love will be our "love of the brethren". Pascal was surely right when he traced three levels of life— the glory of the world with its material resources, the spiritual glory of intellectual achievement, and the final and supreme stage of "charity" that marks the supernatural order of the fellowship of grace.[16] But we must not think of that highest level as one in which only God's spiritual aristocracy may claim a place. Bishop King, of Lincoln, once wrote to a friend on the birth of his first child in these terms: "Love, I believe, *descends*. Parents love their children more than children can their parents, so that children can only enter into the fulness of the parents' love by becoming parents themselves. This is a wonderful true law, running down to the love which animals have for their young, and then running up to the endless, unchangeable, ineffable, knowledge—surpassing love of our Father which is in heaven".[17] Our feet may stand on but the lowest rung of that *scala caritatis*, but like the patriarch in his vision, we can see God at its highest.

[16] *Pensées, De Jésus Christ*, XLI (Faugère's ed. II. pp. 530ff.; Brunschvicg's ed. pp. 695ff.). I owe the reference to my colleague, A. J. D. Farrer.

[17] *Spiritual Letters of Edward King* (ed. by B. W. Randolph), p. 50 (under date 1877).

CHAPTER XII

SOLVITUR PATIENDO

THERE was a famous puzzle of antiquity known as "Achilles and the tortoise". If they were to race, with the tortoise starting from a point ahead of Achilles, how could Achilles ever catch up to him? Whilst Achilles was running to the point from which the tortoise started, the tortoise would get another start, and so on continually. Diogenes replied by showing in practice that the tortoise *could* be overtaken, and so gave rise to the saying "solvitur ambulando" [1]—the answer lies in doing it. We may apply that famous saying to our subject in the form of "solvitur patiendo"—the answer to the most difficult problems of suffering is to be found through bearing it (in the right way). We may be unable to solve the mystery of suffering intellectually, and yet we may *live* through it into the light. There is a profound remark of the philosopher Wittgenstein, to the effect that when we have answered all the scientific questions that could be put,

[1] Professor Claude Jenkins, in a written communication to me, traces the *Latin* phrase to the *Artis Logicae Rudimenta* of Henry Aldrich (1647–1710); see p. 143 of the 1862 edition.

SUFFERING HUMAN AND DIVINE

the problem of life itself remains. Certainly no other question remains, and this very fact supplies the answer—the problem is solved by the disappearance of the problem.[2] The man who has been enabled to face suffering triumphantly has certainly solved one of the fundamental problems of life, though he can never satisfactorily put his solution into words. When Isaac Newton's claim to the discovery of the calculus was challenged, someone sent him a problem that could not be solved without it. He returned the solution next day; that was enough.

In the course of this book, we have been examining one by one the chief things that can be said about suffering, and the chief attempts to explain it. Yet every reader must have felt a certain aridity and inadequacy in some or all of these successive stages of explanation. Suffering is an experience which can absorb all the faculties of mind and body and concentrate them upon the single point of something to be suffered. No abstract argument can cope with it. All that our arguments can do is to remove some of the intellectual difficulties and perhaps prepare us for that act of will in which with resolution and faith we triumph over it. In this closing chapter it is the practical endurance of suffering which concerns us.

Suffering is the common lot and all the devices of man are unable to make him completely immune

[2] *Tractatus Logico-Philosophicus*, p. 186.

from it. Sooner or later, it tracks out our footsteps and discovers our hiding-place. Literature often dwells on this inexorable pursuit, whether it be interpreted as the meaningless operation of a blind fate or bad luck or as the fulfilment of divine purpose, whether it be regarded as penalty or privilege, whether it be acute in the temporary torture of body or mind, or spread over life as physical privation or spiritual discontent. The ancient Book of Ecclesiastes dwells on the weariness and sorrows of life, where "there is one event to all", and reaches a pessimistic and agnostic conclusion even within the conventions of religion. Omar Khayyam—as interpreted by Fitzgerald—sees in the wine-cup the chief escape from destiny, if forgetfulness can be called escape:—

> "The Moving Finger writes; and having writ,
>   Moves on: nor all your Piety nor Wit
>   Shall lure it back to cancel half a Line,
>   Nor all your Tears wash out a Word of it."

On the other hand, Keats' "Song of the Indian Maid" finds a deeper if unexplained contentment in sorrow than in the revelry of Bacchus and his crew, whilst Francis Thompson's "Hound of Heaven" transforms the pursuit of man by suffering into the pursuit by an ultimate Love:

> "All which thy child's mistake
>   Fancies as lost, I have stored for thee at home."

SUFFERING HUMAN AND DIVINE

One of the most suggestive of the literary illustrations
occurs in the thirtieth psalm, verse 5—"Weeping may
come in to lodge at even, but at morn there is a ring-
ing cry of joy." The thought is of the transient guest,
who claims the right of hospitality and must be admitted by the Oriental custom based on the necessi-
ties of the desert, even though he be an enemy. Probably without any consciousness of this verse, its
thought has been worked out in Aubrey de Vere's fine
sonnet, which makes the best commentary on it:—

> "Count each affliction, whether light or grave,
> God's messenger sent down to thee: do thou
> With courtesy receive him; rise and bow;
> And, ere his shadow pass thy threshold, crave
> Permission first his heavenly feet to lave;
> Then lay before him all thou hast; allow
> No cloud of passion to usurp thy brow,
> Or mar thy hospitality; no wave
> Of mortal tumult to obliterate
> The soul's marmoreal calmness: Grief should be,
> Like joy, majestic, equable, sedate;
> Confirming, cleansing, raising, making free;
> Strong to consume small troubles; to commend
> Great thoughts, grave thoughts, thoughts lasting
> to the end."

That might be called Stoicism, but it has been bap-
tized into the Christian faith, and has become confident that the seeming anger of God is but for a

moment, whilst in His favour is the whole of life.
Doubtless such confidence in the love of God is often
reinforced by a number of humanistic motives, the
proper pride in a true dignity under affliction, the
momentum of a persistent purpose to carry on and
win through, the thought of others and of the effect
which our behaviour will have upon them. These re-
inforcements are by no means to be despised, even
from the standpoint of a religious faith. Moreover
they do enable many a man without it to keep a brave
front, to check self-pitying complaint, to lessen the
sympathetic suffering of others. But we are not using
the whole of the resources open to us until we interpret the unwelcome guest as the divine ambassador,
and listen to his challenge, not as an unwelcome in-
terruption to the pleasures of life, but as an invitation
to rise to a higher level of living. In the Jewish story
of Esther, in spite of all its malignant nationalism,
there is a fine example of such disguised embassy. To
the young queen in her youth and beauty and with
the cup of enjoyment held to her lips, there comes
the grim figure of her kinsman Mordecai, clad in sackcloth and ashes, and urging her to imperil life itself
on behalf of her kinsfolk: "who knoweth whether
thou art not come to the kingdom for such a time
as this?"[3] She accepts the message as from God. One

[3] IV. 14.

of the secrets of high living is just that—to penetrate through the disguise of sackcloth and ashes into the divine purpose and the human opportunity. To the Christian faith at its best belongs this secret. Whatever be the affliction, it does not imply a situation that has escaped from the weak hands of God, but is an event that is controlled by His purpose and interpretable, though at long last, in the light of a divine love from which nothing can separate us. The revelation of a deeper meaning for life, given through suffering when so interpreted, can take many forms and have many applications. In the psalm to which reference has been made, the suffering of the psalmist (probably through sickness) broke up the self-complacency which had said in full health and prosperity, "I shall never be moved". Such self-complacency lies at the heart of most of us, even if it does not show itself in vain boasting and petty vanities. In proportion to our success in life we are apt to exalt our own share in obtaining it, and to infer our adequacy against all that would shake other men. Such wrong and foolish pride in ourselves is alien to, indeed incompatible with, any true religion in the Biblical sense. The Hebrew prophets, notably Isaiah, constantly rebuke the pride of man and confine fellowship with God to the humble and lowly in spirit—a testimony which is caught up and continued in the

Beatitudes. But do many of us learn real humility except through humiliation—without disappointment, failure, suffering? Until we are proved incomplete in ourselves, we shall not be conscious of the need of God.

A notable instance of the power of suffering to purge the soul of its pride and to bring it back to the fundamental humility of the true Christian faith is supplied by the French poet, François Coppée (1842–1908). He had abandoned the conventional piety of his youth and had lived the life of many another, without God, through all his literary achievement. Then, at the age of fifty-six, came acute suffering and the humbling of his pride. As he read the Gospel, he writes, "I have seen truth shine like a star, I have felt it beat like a heart". He has told the story of his conversion to genuine faith in his book, *La bonne Souffrance,* which consists of articles written during his illness and convalescence. Underneath the veil of Gallic sentiment and in the form of Catholic piety, we have the familiar experience of the recovery of childlike humility. The word of Jesus brought him, as he says with evident sincerity, to love his suffering, for it brought back to him the lost art of prayer.

If we would see the same experience expressed by one who was not only a literary artist, but also a profound thinker, we may turn to Pascal's "Prayer for

the Profitable Use of Sickness".[4] As a document for
the interpretation of suffering, this "prayer" is well
worth careful study, for it gathers together some of
the great realities of saintly devotion. Its dominant
thought is the reference of every event in life to God,
including this present bodily affliction. He accepts it
as a penalty for his misuse of health—may he not misuse his sickness! Let it be a prelude to the last judgment, to that separation from life which death will
bring. No "means of grace" can give grace, which
must be the gift of God Himself; let God with whom
he is now face to face restore his heart and complete
the work begun in him, that he may freely love God
for Himself. Let the inner suffering of repentance
spring from and correspond to the outer suffering of
the body, a penitent sorrow that he had used health as
a good for himself, and not for God. His thought has
not been God's as expressed in the Beatitudes. Now he
would enter into that fellowship with the sufferings
of Christ in which he may say, "No longer I, but
Christ suffers in me". So shall the first step of suffering without consolation lead to the second step of
suffering with divine consolation, and this to the third
step of true blessedness without suffering. As the Lord

[4] *Pensées*, in Prosper Faugère's edition of 1844, Vol. I, pp. 65-77; in
Brunschvicg's edition, pp. 56-66. It was written, according to some authorities,
at the age of twenty-four. Others put it ten years later.

was known to His disciples by the marks of His suffering, so now let the disciple be known to his Lord, as having entered into the fellowship of His sufferings.

Mr Aldous Huxley, in a recent book [5] criticizes Pascal's attitude towards sickness on the ground that it makes sickness "the truly Christian condition", whereas it may create as many temptations as it removes, since it tends to induce egoism, though he admits an element of truth in its reminder that "the things of this world" are not so important as we are apt to think. He can hardly have studied the prayer just outlined. Pascal explicitly asks to be saved from missing the opportunity of his sickness to grow in grace; he knows perfectly well that sickness can do nothing automatically for anyone. We all know that suffering can brutalize or produce the querulous invalid suggested by the criticism. The truth is that nothing happening from without can do anything for us or against us, independently of our attitude towards it. Suffering, like other phases of our experience, is at most an opportunity for a new experience, not the mechanical provision of one. To be deprived of the health and strength and comfort which have enabled us to be content with ourselves gives us the occasion to ask and perhaps discover what we are without a favourable environment. It is, in fact, a

[5] *Ends and Means*, p. 304.

caricature of Pascal's view of life to say that for him "sickness is the truly Christian condition"; in point of fact, he elsewhere says [6] that sicknesses impair judgment and the senses, and he classes them amongst the sources of human error. It was not a sick mind which pulverized Jesuit casuistry in the *Provincial Letters*.

A further discovery to be made is that all suffering, whether of mind or body, can be the gateway of entrance into larger sympathy with others. Here again, we have to emphasize the fact that there is nothing automatic in this possible effect of suffering. A sufferer may be so absorbed in his suffering that he has little or no thought for the pains of other men. Even if he has, he may indulge himself with the sentimentality of a "philanthropy" which goes hand in hand with callous disregard of the discomfort or privation he is directly causing to those who minister to him. Suffering does indeed provide the data on which imagination can work, and imagination is necessary, even for the comprehension of the Golden Rule. But it is only too easy to go as far as that, and do nothing about it, to indulge in a luxury of sentimentalism which flatters our egoism, and has no product in the will.

Whilst genuine sympathy with the suffering of

[6] *Pensées*, in Brunschvicg's ed. p. 3'68:—"*Nous avons un autre principe d'erreur, les maladies. Elles nous gâtent le jugement et le sens.*"

others requires some experience of suffering, it is not, of course, true to say that it requires a similar experience. No doubt, it is a great help to the imagination seeking to penetrate into the mystery of another's inner life, to have passed through circumstances externally similar. Even so, the reaction within may be quite different, and it is with the reaction that we are concerned. The novelist and the dramatist are not limited in their effective sympathy with their characters by autobiographical material. Just as the well-trained mind can apply itself successfully to a very wide range of enquiry, so the well-trained imagination can enter into the secrets of many lives; all that is needed is enough experience to supply the training. This is the justification for the New Testament statement that Jesus "hath been in all points tempted like as we are, yet without sin".[7] In a strictly verbal sense, that would obviously not be true, for the particular circumstances of the life of Jesus exempted Him from many trials to which we are exposed. But it is true that "He learned obedience by the things which He suffered" [8] and so entered into the capacity to sympathize with all kinds of suffering.

Whilst there is a biological "sympathy" underlying man's social relations (visible, for example, in the

[7] Heb. IV. 15.
[8] V. 8.

"psychology of the crowd"), and an imaginative sympathy with the individual sufferer which has no moral significance, the higher growth of conscious and purposive sympathy requires the breaking-up of much hard soil. Here the incidence of suffering takes an important part, indeed, it is hard to see what other plough can cut the necessary furrows. We may take the classical example given in Coleridge's poem, "The Ancient Mariner", which is all the better for our purpose because it is so familiar. Here we have the story of the man whose thoughtless and cruel shooting of the albatross brings great suffering upon himself and his companions. At first, as the poet's significant marginal comments tell us, "he despiseth the creatures of the calm", but at length Nature works her gracious influence upon him, and the sight of the beauty and happiness of the water-snakes which he watches in the moon-light, wins from him a blessing unawares. He has begun to sympathize with other existences than his own, because suffering has broken up his hardness, and given him a new opportunity. His final penance is a privilege, for it is "to teach, by his own example, love and reverence to all things that God made and loveth". Suffering has opened the door into an avenue of life where may be won that prize of learning love which it is the great purpose of "life, with all it yields of joy and woe, and hope and fear" to offer us the chance of winning.⁹ A man who really believes this will thank God for any shock of physical or spiritual suffering which opened his eyes to his true relation to others, and began to teach him that "all our doings without charity are nothing worth".

If suffering is thus essential to the growth of character and to a man's right relation to his social environment, it is not less essential to that for which character exists in the present world-order, viz., the actualization of truth. This fact is epitomized in the well-known transition of meaning in the word "martyr" from its original force of "witness" to that of "sufferer". That transition is due to the fact that suffering for a conviction is at once the strongest proof of sincerity to oneself and the most convincing witness to other men. We see the transition taking place in the New Testament, where the Greek word *martures* means "declaratory witnesses" in Acts I. 8 ("Ye shall be my witnesses") and "suffering witnesses" or martyrs in Rev. XVII. 6 ("the blood of the martyrs of Jesus", R.V.). We saw in the Old Testament that Job was such a martyr-witness to the reality of disinterested religion. One of Paul's most striking metaphors—and his metaphors are worthy of his adventures—brings out the force of the word without actually using it. In I Cor. IV. 9, he writes, "God

⁹ See the opening paragraphs of Ch. IV.

hath set forth us the apostles last of all as men doomed
to death; for we are made a spectacle *(theatron)*
unto the world, both to angels and to men". He is
contrasting the superficial Christians of Corinth with
those who have borne the burden and faced the peril
of Christian witness, and he is thinking of the amphitheatre. To feel the full force of that metaphor, we
need to visit the ruins of some Roman amphitheatre
and to stand in the arena, with the stone benches rising all around us filled to the eye of imagination with
their former spectators. Paul and his companions are
the gladiators of God—the rest are those who watch
their struggles in comfort. But the apostle looks up
past the rings of visible onlookers to the open sky
above. He sees other spectators in that invisible world,
deeply concerned with the issue, and he draws strength
from their silent sympathy with his sufferings.

It is easy for us, who watch the world's great men
in the arena of public affairs, to think of ourselves
simply as spectators. But the common lot of suffering
sooner or later claims *us* also in our smaller world. Invisible hands thrust us down into the arena of that
little world in which ordinary men live. Here we, too,
are compelled to play our part, and show ourselves
brave or cowardly. Every one of us, in the time of
suffering, has his opportunity to bear witness to the
unseen things through the seen quality of his demean-

our. Our arena is a small one, but it is none the less real and influential over other lives. In our particular struggle we may be victorious or defeated, so far as some particular issue is concerned. That is a secondary thing as compared with the quality of the struggle, the attitude of the sufferer, which can transform apparent defeat into real victory. On such things of daily experience depends the moral and religious quality of the whole world, and every one of us, however utterly passive his lot may be in appearance, can be really active in contribution to the spiritual forces of the universe. "The veil of the flesh, when it is made more transparent by suffering, lets through the light of another world with greater brilliance." [10]

This kind of witness-bearing is open to the humblest sufferer, for it may consist simply in showing that, like Job, we can "fear God for nought". But the greatest of all sources of comfort and strength in suffering is found in the relation of its human forms to the divine. We have seen, again and again, our inability to explain the incidence of all suffering, and to defend its justice, from the standpoint of the individual life. But here we have to think of the living relation of one personality with another, the human with the divine, a relation which goes deeper than any abstract argument about it can ever do. Clear

[10] T. H. Hughes, *The Philosophic Basis of Mysticism*, p. 226.

consciousness of this is apparent in the conversations of the Upper Room, just before the crucifixion, as recorded in the Fourth Gospel. The disciples successively seize their last opportunity of putting questions to their Master.[11] Peter asks, "Whither goest thou? . . . why cannot I follow thee even now?" Thomas asks, "How know we the way?" Philip says, "Show us the Father and it sufficeth us". Judas (not Iscariot) asks, "What is come to pass that thou wilt manifest thyself unto us, and not unto the world?" Now the significant thing is that to none of these questions does Jesus give a directly informative reply, but to them all he suggests a relation to Himself which is an effective answer. Peter is reminded of the cost of loyalty and the weakness of the flesh and of the spirit in face of peril. Thomas is reminded that discipleship to Christ is already the way to the unseen world. Philip is bidden to find in what he has already seen in the Son the true and sufficient revelation of the Father. Judas (not Iscariot) is called to turn his thoughts from the passing Passover crowds, and to concentrate on the one condition of receiving the Christian revelation—love for the Lord. Many questions and one answer—Jesus Himself.

If we would know what kind of personality, what conditions and qualities of life are His with whom the

[11] XIII. 36—XIV. 24.

disciple is thus brought into relation, we do well to
follow the advice of both Harnack [12] and Montefiore [13] and turn to the Beatitudes. The former tells
us that when we are in doubt as to what Jesus stands
for, we should sink our thought deep again into the
Beatitudes; the latter says that they teach the one
thing needful, as distinct from all that is external and
institutional, civic and political, aesthetic and intellectual, however legitimate and necessary these and
our progressive attempts to realize them may be. Now
the Beatitudes as given in Matthew [14] utter a blessing
on both grief and persecution; if, as is probable, the
form given to the first and fourth by Luke (VI. 20,
21) is original, we must add poverty and hunger.
There can be no doubt that Jesus set a value on suffering which is in direct antithesis to the common
judgments of men. It is no wonder that F. W. Rob-
ertson, writing of a time of sorrow and distress in his
own life, could think of this antithesis, and say of the
Beatitudes, "They fell upon my heart like music." [15]

The same insistence on the place of suffering in
the Christian life is expressed in the solemn warning
spoken at Caesarea Philippi:—"If any man would
come after me, let him deny himself and take up his

[12] *Das Wesen des Christentums*, p. 47.
[13] *Hibbert Journal*, Oct., 1929, p. 109.
[14] V. 3-12.
[15] *Life and Letters*, Vol. II, p. 193.

cross and follow me".[16] That was the supreme mark
of the true disciple in the contemporary conditions,
and its principle surely abides. We must not water it
down into what is sometimes called "cross-bearing",
when we seek to dignify our petty annoyances with a
high-sounding name. It denoted then, as it still primarily denotes, the loyalty to Christ which was so
complete that nothing could stand in the way of
obedience, and that the price of inevitable suffering
would be readily paid for the sake of the fellowship
with Him. At the same time, we may justly extend
the principle to all suffering which is faced in the
spirit of Christ Himself, that is in the spirit of submission to the Father's will. For it is true to say with
Bourget, "nothing is lost when we make an offering
of it".[17] At any given moment of life, whatever the
cause of our affliction or its dire extent, we can make
a new start by such consecration of the suffering.
Whatever is lost, *this* remains—that we may hope to
enter into a closer knowledge of God in Christ
through the right endurance of our suffering.

Can we say more than that? Can we venture to
speak of ourselves in apostolic terms, as filling up that
which remains of the sufferings of Christ? Yes, if we
share in the apostle's assumption of a union with
Christ so real and so close that he lived, and yet not

[16] Mark VIII. 34.
[17] *Le Sens de la Mort*, p. 310.

he, but Christ lived in him, so that the consecrated suffering of the Christian becomes the continued suffering of the Body of Christ. We have here a truly Christian and most inspiring thought. Something has been said about it in the chapters dealing with the redemptive value of suffering and with the fellowship of suffering, human and divine. The sacrificial Love of God has its unique historical manifestation on Calvary. But Calvary cannot be detached from all that it means in the lives of men—all its dimmer adumbrations in earlier days, all its resultant renewals in the centuries since. How much it would lighten the burden of otherwise unexplained suffering, if we could feel that, in some real sense, we, who are called to share the creative activity of God by the exercise of our freedom, are called also to share in the completion of His redemptive work by the loyal endurance of suffering *with Him!* One thing is certain to Christian faith, and every experience of suffering can reinforce its certainty—that the ultimate strength to bear, and the ultimate answer to all the questions which suffering raises is to be found in the ever-deepening assurance of the love of God. As Horatius Bonar's great hymn on the divine love sings:—

> "O heavenly Love, how precious still,
> In days of weariness and ill,
> In nights of pain and helplessness,
> To heal, to comfort and to bless!"

This interpretative principle is confirmed by every successful application of it. Each step of the journey taken with Him becomes a new proof that He will see us through whatever remains. The great apocalyptic vision of the coronation festival of the King [18] when He will remove the veil of the mourner and wipe away the tears from every face, destroying the last enemy, death, becomes more than the dream of a visionary, in the light of this growing experience. The uncrossed threshold, the lost opportunities of earth, can bring no bitterness to one who has learnt to say, "I would rather stand on the threshold of the house of my God" than to dwell anywhere on earth.[19]

Such a faith is not selfishly individualistic. However triumphant it may be in the single life, it carries the burden of other lives, lives perhaps without such consolations, without God and without hope. But there is also the confidence that the resources of God are not exhausted by what we yet know, and that the life we live here is only a fragment of something larger. If we know, as Christians, how little we have attained and how far we have yet to go, here or hereafter, we shall not be despondent as to those who seem to have missed so much that has been given to us, and not least, this Christian faith itself. We shall believe,

[18] Is. XXV. 6-8.
[19] Ps. LXXXIV. 10.

with Bishop King, that "shadows are made by sunlight above".[20] We shall dare to believe that those who
seem to have missed most can still cry, "Hast thou
but one blessing, O my Father?" and find His other
blessings in the new conditions of another world.

In the *Solvitur Patiendo* of the Christian there are
always at least three elements, on which our final emphasis should fall, especially as they will serve to gather
up and focus much that this book has endeavoured to
say. The first of these is the need for the persistent
purpose. Towards the end of James Elroy Flecker's
"Hassan" there are some simple words which gain
their essential meaning from the momentum of the
whole play. They are spoken by Ishak, the Caliph's
minstrel, for himself, and for the utterly broken
Hassan, as they forsake the horrible suffering and callous brutality of the world in which they have lived
and take the Golden Road to Samarkand:—

"We are the Pilgrims, master; we shall go
  Always a little further: it may be
  Beyond that last blue mountain barred with snow,
  Across that angry or that glimmering sea."

It is good to have the worn metaphor of our life as a
pilgrimage re-minted and given fresh circulation, for
it is an essential thought of Biblical religion and of

[20] *Spiritual Letters*, p. 157.

Christian faith. That is one reason why Bunyan's book will always hold its own, and especially for those who have learnt to read the author's own spiritual pilgrimage in "Grace Abounding" between the lines of "The Pilgrim's Progress". The pilgrim has always these two characteristics; he wills to let go and he wills to go on. He has acquired the spirit of detachment, the spirit of the celebration of the Jewish Passover, eaten with loins girded and feet shod and staff in hand, ready for the journey. For him the sorrow of a great bereavement, the suffering of some bitter disappointment, may help, as a veritable "goad of God", to detach him from the past and to urge him forward on his journey. The apostle was reminded of such a goad, on the journey to Damascus that became a spiritual pilgrimage, and we may use the term to describe "each sting that bids nor sit nor stand but go". It may even be, as Robert Louis Stevenson suggested in *The Celestial Surgeon*, "a killing sin" that "stabs my spirit broad awake" for the journey before me. A pilgrim may often have to say of his suffering what is said in the "Psalms of Solomon":—[21]

"When my soul slumbered (being far) from the Lord....
He goaded me, as a horse is goaded, that I might watch for Him."

[21] XVI. 1-4.

The second necessary element of the *Solvitur Patiendo* is that, to the "letting go" and the "going on", there is added a "looking up". We can hardly expect to maintain the persistent purpose against all the shocks and changes of life unless it is continually strengthened or renewed by the vision of some goal beyond ourselves, some loyalty that takes us out of ourselves and helps us to forget or at least overcome the toil and suffering of the way. Here a sentence from the Mishnah may memorably epitomize the truth, if we are allowed to allegorize it. In the ritual for the daily offering in the Temple, which began before the dawn, it was the duty of a solitary priest to go in the darkness into the inner enclosure of the altar, to clear away the ashes of the fire which was kept continually burning. It was the rule that "none went in with him and he carried no lamp, but *he walked in the light of the altar fire*". I have sometimes tried to imagine what Rembrandt might have made of such a scene, but here my thought is that every man who goes on doing his duty in the darkness of suffering will be walking by the light of *some* altar fire, though none but himself may know of it, and perhaps not he himself.

The third and last element of the Christian *Solvitur Patiendo* is the full and frank recognition that the inner peace for which we are all craving is not the peace of escape from the sufferings of life, but the peace of a victory won in their very midst and through their endurance. I remember very vividly how this elementary truth was brought home to me in a valley of Tyrol. A friend and I stood late one night on the little bridge over the stream at Prutz. The village was asleep; all around us were the snow-covered hills gleaming in the moonlight, and the only sound was the ripple of the stream beneath our feet. One of us said to the other how far we were in this valley of peace from all the sin and sorrow and suffering of the world. It was then that we caught sight of a crucifix, unnoticed before and fixed to the bridge. The sudden sight of the Sufferer's face, clear in the moonlight, was unforgettable. It seemed as though we heard a voice speaking to us and saying, "O foolish men, to think that peace is ever found in seclusion from the world, or in flight from its suffering. Here, on the Cross, is My peace, the peace which I give unto you". *Solvitur Patiendo*.

SOME BOOKS ABOUT SUFFERING

JAMES HINTON, *The Mystery of Pain*, 1866.

FRANÇOIS COPPÉE, *La Bonne Souffrance*, 1898.

R. C. MOBERLY, *Sorrow, Sin and Beauty*, 1903.

A. S. PEAKE, *The Problem of Suffering in the Old Testament*, 1904.

W. R. SORLEY and others, *The Elements of Pain and Conflict in Human Life*, 1916.

E. W. JOHNSON, *Suffering, Punishment and Atonement*, 1919.

T. B. KILPATRICK, "Suffering" (in the *Encyclopaedia of Religion and Ethics*, Vol. XII, pp. 1-10), 1921.

F. VON HÜGEL, "Suffering and God" (address delivered in 1921 and published in *Essays and Addresses, Second Series*), 1926.

J. K. MOZLEY, *The Impassibility of God*, 1926.

H. R. MACKINTOSH, *The Christian Experience of Forgiveness*, 1927.

B. R. BRASNETT, *The Suffering of the Impassible God*, 1928.

M. C. D'ARCY, *The Pain of this World and the Providence of God*, 1935.

J. S. WHALE, *The Christian Answer to the Problem of Evil*, 1936.

GEOFFREY GORDON, *The Life of Mastery*, 1938.

INDEX

INDEX

Freedom and the idea of a fall, 79; human, and responsibility for suffering, 104

Frustration, not attributable to God, 148

Future life, 131-132

God, and the idea of the Absolute, 154-155; and the problem of time, 150-153; discovery of, in pain, 13-14; extent of His responsibility for man's suffering, 104; guidance of, in human life, 128-129; impassibility of, 144; love of, 219; passibility of, 145; providence of, 129; responsibility for suffering, 138; revealed in Nature, 9-10; self-limitation of, 149-150; triumphant love of, 132

Grace, the expression of suffering, 180

Greek thought and the interpretation of Christ, 144

Group and individual, 54-55; consciousness, 54

Guidance, infallible, 128

Guilt, sense of, and suffering, 71

Healing ministry of Jesus, 119

Hinton, James: "The Mystery of Pain", 41, 196

History, meaning of, transformed by fellowship with God, 198-200; providential control of, 110

Holiness and effect of sin, 177-180

Hosea, knowledge of God through suffering, 42-43

Humility, learnt through suffering, 207

Ignorance, cost of, to human race, 107

Individual, debt of, to society, 59; emergence of, 55; extent and nature of responsibility of, 76; inheritance of good and evil, 57; "rights" of, in society, 54; rights and obligations of, 56-57

Ingratitude, sin of, 59

Instinct and the exercise of reason, 51-52

Jeremiah, knowledge of God through suffering, 43

Jesus, and belief in spirits, 81; and the principle of retribution, 35; and the sacrificial principle of suffering, 45; and the world of Nature, 99-102; attitude to history and contemporary politics, 116-119; healing ministry of, 118-119; humanity of, 145; love of, revealing God's love, 157; personality of, 141; place of, in Christian faith, 140-141; relation of disciples to Him, 215-216; suffering of, 141-142; two-nature doctrine of, 156-157; victory over moral evil, 169; see also *the Cross*

Job, book of, 4, 35, 37, 41

Kingdom of God, 118-120

Limitation causing suffering: self-limitation of God, 149-150

Literature, inheritance of, 58

Loom, as figure of life, 10, 112.

Love, cost of, 155-156; of God, 199-200, 219; place of, in life of individual, 49-50

Man, creative power of, 134-136.

"Martyr", 40-42, 213-214

Miracle, 89-91

Moral discipline of suffering, 18

INDEX

Moral evil, actuality of, 176; and death, 77-78; and suffering, 3, 65-66, 74-75; and suffering, the Crucifixion, 65-66; and the suffering of Nature, 78-79; as "vice", 69; the abuse of freedom, 66; victory of the Cross over, 169; see also *Evil*

Motive, and standard of values, 129-130

Nature, 9-10 (and Ch. VI); a source of spiritual healing, 93; and providence, 99-102; attitude of Jesus to, 199-102; corporate structure of, 96-98; dynamic quality of, 93-96; purpose of, 94-95; regularity of, 87-93; revealing God, 9-10, 14; suffering of, and moral evil, 78-79; the laws of, Ch. VI

Old Testament, rise of the problem of suffering in, 31

Pain, avoidance of, as motive, 20; Nature's danger signal, 19; revealing God, 14; see also *Suffering*

Pascal, attitude to sickness, 207-209

Passibility of God; philosophical difficulties, 145-154

Paul, and the principle of retribution, 35, 45; and the witness of suffering, 213-214; fellowship in Christ's suffering, 190; relation of sin and death, 76-77

Pessimistic interpretation of history, 113-116

Prayer, 127

Probationary and evidential principle of suffering, in the Old Testament, 39-42

Progress, slowness of, a cause of suffering, 105-106

Providence, a personal relation between God and man, 129-130; and Nature, 99-102; control of, in history, 110-113; "special", 126-129

Psycho-therapy, 29-30

Punishment, theories of, 71-74

Purpose, need of, 221-222; of God in human life, 206; the key to life, 116

Reade, Winwood: "The Martyrdom of Man", 106

Redemption, Protestant doctrine of, 166-167

Religion, cost of ignorance in, 107-108

Repentance, 171; inadequacy of, 175

Responsibility of individual, 76

Resurrection, doctrine of, 46-47

Retribution, idea of, in Paul, 45

Retributive theory of punishment, 71-74; of suffering, 34-36, 185-186

Revelational principle of suffering, 42-46

Rights of individual, cost of attainment, 56-57; in society, 54

Sacrifice, nature of, in the Old Testament, 43-45

Sacrificial principle of suffering, 43-46

St Teresa, experience and doctrine of redemption, 164

Self-sacrifice and social morality, 61

Selfishness and its issues in social life, 51; and sin, 51

Servant of the Lord, the, 40-41, 43

Shakespeare: "King Lear", 1-3, 115

Sin and selfishness, 50-51; as moral evil in relation to God, 66; destroys man's higher nature, 80; its effect on holiness, 177-180; transformation of, in atonement, 183

INDEX

Social interpretation of suffering, 21-22

Spirit, Holy, continuing the work of Christ, 159-160

Spirit world, belief in, 81

Spiritual life, possibility of "law" in, 88-89

Stoicism and suffering, 27-28

Stoics and the natural world, 91-92

Suffering, accompanies awakening of conscience, 70-71; and character, 21; and moral evil, 3, 66, 74-75; as the will of God, 12; disciplinary value of, 36-39; eschatological principle of, 46-48; explanations of, in Bible, 185-186 (and Ch. III); fact of, 6; futility of, partly explained in social progress, 189-190; human, its value for God, 193; human, redemptive value of, 190-191; levels of explanation, 18; man's capacity to transform meaning of, 13-15; ministry through, 24; Nature's danger signal, 19-20; outside Christian faith, its value for God, 194; personal reaction to, 11-12; probationary and evidential principle, 39-42; retributive, idea of, in the

Old Testament, 34-36; revelational principle of, in the Old Testament, 42-43; rise of problem, in the Old Testament, 31-34; sacrificial principle of, in the Old Testament, 41; social interpretation of, 21-22; spiritual, 70; spiritual more intense than physical, 1-2, 7; the cost of service to mankind, 60; transformation of, 195-198, 204; voluntarily accepted by God, 180; see also *Pain*

Superstition and its cost, 107-110

Sympathy, 188-189; enriched by suffering, 210-214

Time, problem of, 150-155

Tragedy, transformation of, 5-6

Transformation of evil in the Cross, 171-172; of evil into good, 193-194; of sin in atonement, 183; of suffering, 195-198, 204; of the meaning of events, 134-136; of the meaning of suffering, 13-15

Values, standard of, 129-131

Witness-bearing, 213-214